JELLY BEAN F

Serial homicide is not for

JELLY BEAN EFFECT

First edition. February 27, 2024.

ISBN: 979-8223453239

Written by Johnny Taute.

Also by Johnny Taute

Jelly Bean Effect

Johnny Taute

Proof reading by Carmen Harper

All correspondence to
bluandyoung@gmail.com

"The Wedding-Guest sat on a stone:
He cannot choose but hear;
And thus spake on that ancient man,
The bright-eyed Mariner."
- The Rime of the Ancient Mariner by Samuel Coleridge

-ONE-

†

SANTA BARBARA. USA. 2003.

Tonight, the tempest keeps pounding heavy surf toward the Carpinteria shoreline, causing a sizable buildup of sand at the harbor mouth. The lights of the Coast Village road villas in affluent Montecito, flicker in unison with the rhythmicity of the swaying power lines.

Jordan Worthington nestles in front of the gas fire in her cozy living room, her PowerBook G4 balances on her lap. The western wall of her elegant duplex is adorned with posters of award-winning book covers. On the southern wall, there's a montage of framed family photos. The flat-screen television relays the weather report at a barely audible level.

"The storm system moved across Santa Barbara County more quickly than was anticipated this autumn. Rain clouds swept through, maxing out at five inches in the mountains, propelled by winds gusting to nearly 50mph in some of the passes of the Santa Ynez Mountains-"

Even in the subdued lighting, it is pertinent that Jordan understands the 60-30-10 ratio of hues in decorating, with brilliant white coming in at 60. Her faux mink blanket and chipped Milo mug render the only shade of gray. The steaming beverage is parked on top of a well-read copy of Coleridge's "The Rime of the Ancient Mariner."

As Jordan reviews her work, she reads her typed paragraph on the laptop screen out loud.

"In Africa, darkness provides camouflage to nocturnal predators and lightning exposes them. So what do I fear most; the bright light and thunder or the silent dark brutes?"

Thunder strikes close to the villa and the room turns pitch black! Only the Macbook provides some pale illumination.

Jordan utilizes the screen as a flashlight, as she ascends the staircase. The intermittent lightning strikes distorts her shadow against the hallway wall; a strobed series of frames resembling the dance of a contorted marionette.

Jordan enters her son's bedroom, switches on a baby blue emergency lamp and is relieved to see that her two-year-old son is still fast asleep. She tucks him in again, leaves a kiss on his cheek before returning downstairs.

The house's lights return as well. "Thank you, honey!" She whispers loudly, before collecting the laptop and her thoughts. She pulls the sweater over her knees. Jordan reads along as she types;

"In Africa, night is night! Ink black, moonless, haunting nights. During my recent visit to my native South Africa, I have come to learn that monsters do not lurk in the bush, nor do they conceal themselves underneath our beds."

She takes a sip of Milo.

"They reside in the tortured souls of the children that we neglect. And decades later, the initial childhood trauma in tandem with genetics and abuse, becomes a deviant adult."

She stops to look up at the monochrome wedding portrait of her mother.

"It was murder that made me immigrate; it was a death that made me return. But the victims of a serial killer kept me captive."

-TWO-

†

BOKSBURG, SOUTH AFRICA, 1967.
Boksburg was known for many things in the 1960s: The rise of the Republic, institutionalized repression, the suitcase containing the headless torso of Cathleen Burch which was discovered in the Boksburg lake and angry high-veld thunderstorms.

On such a drenched afternoon, Esther exits an Indian Spaza shop and steps into the soft spray of a subsiding August shower. Pedestrians dash in all directions to find shelter, believing that running in the rain will make them less wet, than walking. Esther enjoys the drops ricocheting off her dark skin. She fills her lungs with the scent of wet earth.

Home! Zulu land!

She makes her way back to the house, where she works as the housekeeper for a widower, Mr. Doep. A hefty bag of maize meal is propped on top of her head, as is the custom of all traditional women when carrying a load. She walks tardily along the line of parked Audi's, BMW's and other German cars. A rushing British Cortina upsets the Reich, as it races past Esther. She ducks behind the body of a Benz as it sends a spray of bedraggled water her way. "*I wanna hold your hand-*" the Beetles profess, blaring past her from behind opaque windows.

Esther lets out an ancient Zulu curse.

As the music subsides, the streets go quiet. Esther is drawn to a familiar sound, but the last descending water makes it difficult to discern where the audio is emanating from.

Do I hear a baby crying?

Esther inspects the parked vehicles on both sides of the narrow suburban road, peeking inside for signs of life, until she notices the red telephone booth.

The rain stops. Like an omen.

The city is secluded. Everyone's inside. The street light winks twice and then closes its eye.

Maybe I heard it wrong?

Esther approaches the cubicle. The glass is fogged up, but she is still able to distinguish some movement on the floor of the telephone booth.

Suddenly, from inside the booth, a baby starts howling. Esther is taken aback by the muffled cry. Ester looks around in desperation for assistance before she places her bag down. Unsure of how to proceed, she wipes away the water from the glass and peers inside.

Can it be?

Ester drags the framed door open. Inside, a frightened 2-year-old Caucasian girl attempts to keep her brother of 6-months from crying. The street light sputter back to life to shine a light on a sad situation.

The girl scurries into a corner, still cradling the wrapped infant. Esther removes the bag from her head and kneels to calm the frightened child. "He is hungry," Esther says while miming a baby drinking from a bottle.

They sit motionless for a while before the girl hands over the baby as well as a bag containing empty bottles and some stained cloth diapers.

They rise. Esther straps the baby on her back and replaces the food parcel on her head. "Rabbits, either I leave you for the rats or I take you to the python," she sighs. "Come." She holds out her hand, inviting the little girl to join her. The child responds.

Hand in hand, they journey back to the Spaza shop, as the skies start to cry once more.

-THREE-

†

E sther hesitates before she steps into a dimly lit, damp kitchen. The olive-colored Formica tops are as scuffed as the lime linoleum floor, and the zink is stacked with greasy pots and plates. Everywhere, large cockroaches scurry and scavenge for morsels of fat.

Doep is a redneck in his late fifties. His thinning, gray, unkempt hair and "lamb chop" sideburns only serve to emphasize his bald top and unmistakable liver spots. He is dressed in a stained yellow vest, which mothballs refuse to protect any longer. The plate of scrambled eggs in front of him, is obscured by his newspaper. He lowers the paper slightly when the soaked trio disturb his peace, cigarette still gripped between discolored fingers. In the corner, a small portable radio plays a happy song. It is Jelly Bean by Eddie Cochran.

> *"Jelly bean, jelly bean*
> *Well that's the name we picked for you*
> *And it fits you to-a-T-"*

An agitated Doep, stares at Esther as she silently presents a tin of baby formula and prepares food for the crying infant.

"I found them in a phone- He is just hungry, baas."

Doep grunts and looks at the fearful girl for some time. The ash breaks off his cigarette and drops onto his food. Without breaking contact, Doep stuffs his mouth full of eggs and shakes the newspaper like wet laundry.

He turns the radio louder to drain out the baby's crying, before he continues reading.

> *"There's a guy who lives in our block*

His name is Curly Carr
Each night he comes around the street
Packin' his guitar,
Stops at jelly bean's house-"

-FOUR-

†

"The fair breeze blew, the white foam flew, The furrow followed free;
We were the first that ever burst into that silent sea."
- Rime of the Ancient Mariner.

PORT ELIZABETH, SOUTH AFRICA, 1997.

The South African Airbus A330's wheels screech down the sunny Port Elizabeth landing strip, as the Indian Ocean blankets the beach under teal and white waves.

Rows of bright white cargo planes wait patiently for their cargo bellies to get filled with flowers, frozen lobster, ostrich meat and skins as well as delectable mushrooms.

Jordan does a quick inspection of her long blond hair and make-up in a pocket mirror, before confidently striding through the arrivals terminal. As always, she is dressed in an immaculate white Coco Chanel suit. Her designer bag matches her shoes, watch, jewelry and the latest Erickson phone. 60-30-10 to the T.

The rubble stop to admire, gossip, shout out her name and wave while some fans snap Polaroid photos of her. A handful of paparazzi is being hassled by airport security.

A porter follows with her luggage.

A tall man dressed in black, continues to escort her. Jordan, uneasy, turns towards him. He passes by, leaving her flushed. She collects herself and shoots for the exit.

A chubby 10-year-old rugrat munching on a bag of jelly beans, spills some of the sweets on the tiles in front of her. The child dives down, almost tripping her up. "Sorry, Auntie."

She manages a smile in the direction of the mother as the sticky, fat little fingers collect blue, green, white and red beans, from the floor.

The boy's stained mouth suggests that the black and yellow candies were the first to perish and may not be his favorite flavors. The spilled colors were saved for last.

He pops a green bean into his mouth while admiring her. "Aunty looks beautiful."

Jordan is thankful for her dark shades, as her eyes betray the disgust she conceals. She briskly sidesteps the child, her strides growing, until she bursts into the open air outside the terminal building. She gasps for air.

Clean, ocean wind!

Her smile returns instantly when she recognizes her brother, David Worth, waiting with outstretched arms. As they hug, Jordan's emotions spill over and she sobs into her brother's shoulder. He holds her tight for a while, as the world continues on its way. "I am sorry. I promised myself I was going to be strong."

David pushes her back to take her in.

"Hey, I am the oldest and you are supposed to cry on my shoulder," she says.

Jordan laughs and dabs her eyes.

"Your part is to be the kindest, most beautiful and most celebrated sister in the whole world, remember? Oh, I have missed you," David tells her.

"And I have the bravest, most fine-looking brother."

David takes the trolley and tips the porter. Jordan turns around to see the dark man exiting the terminal in the distance. "Can we get to the town car, please?"

David pushes the trolley towards the curb. Jordan walks off at a brisk pace. David calls her back. "Your car is on its way." He opens his jacket to reveal his police badge and firearm. "You are safe."

Jordan sighs and rejoins David. He changes the topic. "Gigi was super excited to see you, but it is school break, so Jacqui took her away on holiday- And with Mum's passing-"

Jordan takes his hand. "It's not a great time for anybody. I follow online and it's astounding how much she grows every year. Listen- I can't stay more than a few days- with my book launch coming up- It would be unfair of me to expect her to wait just to see me instead of having fun-"

"Gigi is almost ten." David interrupts. "Next month. The last time you saw her, she was six."

"I know my niece's birthday! Oh man, I am so looking forward to buying her a set of drums!" Jordan plays a rhythm set, on her brother's chest.

"As if she needs to make more noise," he says, smiling and checking his phone. "The driver is almost here."

Jordan strokes his arm. "How are you handling the divorce?"

David manages a smile. "You get to know more about someone at the end of the relationship. But we don't use our child as an instrument of manipulation to resolve our disputes."

"Just as long as your relationship mêlée doesn't impact negatively on your child, Auntie Jordan is happy."

"Oh, big words from a famous writer?" David jokes.

"I am not a writer, I'm a novelist! Have you ever read one of my books?"

"A little bit, I prefer to watch the old Dick Tracey kinda shows when I get the time." He winks. Jordan rotates her shoulders. She looks past David's for any sign of the dark figure, when a Mercedes stops in front of them. David pops the boot. "Better than a town car. Your own chauffeur and security detail!"

Brian Harper steps out of the car, removes his denim jacket, smiles and starts loading her baggage. "Hello Jordan. Good to see you again." He stops packing for a moment. "I am truly sorry for your loss."

Jordan has just had the wind taken out of her and it shows. She quickly retorts. "Brian Harper. What a surprise!" She glances at David, not happy. "You guys are still inseparable, I see."

"Actually, I-" Brian starts, but Jordan feels an inexplicable need to take control. "Are you my bodyguard? My security detail or just the chauffeur? And how's the girlfriend? Sonia, is it?" She steps up to Brian, smirking and removes her sunglasses. "Oh wait, don't tell me-She left you?"

Brian turns and continues stacking the boot. David pulls Jordan away and helps her into the car. "Sonia passed away," David whispers, "she was murdered last year, during a home invasion."

Jordan is totally perplexed. "Shit! Why didn't you tell me this?"

"Because you said that you did not want to know anything about my friends. Remember?"

Jordan punches the back of the car seat and whispers to herself. *Fuck!*

-FIVE-

†

Perched on a dune, Stewart Wilken looks much older than his 31 years. His skin resembles barky cork. Too many bottles opened, every last harmful drop finished and it shows, on every part of his being.

His dark receding hair is clumped into a nondescript wattle-seed and dried-grass motif, a disheveled crown that speaks of a life spent outdoors. Paunchy, abrasive hands, etched with the scars of labor, betray his occupation as a dock worker. They bear witness to the countless hours spent hauling, lifting, and trawling under the harsh sun. He again drags hard on his joint, the rolled amalgamation of tobacco and weed encased in an old newspaper. The makeshift cigarette is a testament to the resourcefulness born of necessity.

The acrid scent of smoke mingles with the salty tang of the coastal breeze as he inhales deeply, seeking solace in the temporary reprieve it offers.

When he eventually exhales, the smoke dissipates instantly in the strong coastal wind. Port Elizabeth isn't dubbed the *"Windy City"* for no reason.

Stewart, caught between the past and the present, finds himself perched on the edge of his own story in a futile attempt at escaping the charge that weigh on him- the burdens etched into the lines on his face and the weariness in his eyes.

Wuané is dwarfed by her father's stocky frame, where she sits next to him. Next to him, not close, in silence while watching the waves break against Shark Rock Pier. The 10-year-old girl is dressed in a hand-me-down, white and blue checkered tracksuit top, sporting her favorite friend; Minnie Mouse.

Stewart sucks the good shit from the last inch of the joint, spits out a seed and flicks the rest into a rock pool. "You must think I am a fucked-up dad? And Hey? And-, well, you'll still see-"

He looks down at her stark face. The breeze transports the sounds of joyful tourists, making memories on the pier, towards their somber conversation. "I am sorry Wuané, I never learned how to- And you know, and in this shit world. And until you were born- And then geezas! I sound stupid when I speak." Stewart forces a grin.

Then his expression turns serious. "But I didn't want you to have the same kak as I- And I have to take you away from them. That's why I have to hide you."

-SIX-

†

The silver Mercedes C-class sweeps down Marine Drive and past the Shark Rock Pier, as another busload of Asian tourists disembark. Brian is behind the wheel, David riding shotgun.

David points to the pier. "I used to take Mum to the pier, to serenade. She would sing Sinatra songs into the wind. There she could sing off-tune and out loud, without anyone hearing her," he smiles and shakes his head. Brian turns the radio volume down more, inviting conversation from Jordan's side.

Declined.

Deep in thought and shame, Jordan desires nothing more than to escape to her hotel. David feels compelled to break the uncomfortable silence. "Mum loved it here. She said it is as beautiful as a bible verse. A psalm by David."

Jordan smiles in an effort to somehow comfort her brother, when he turns towards her.

"She would sit at her window for hours, drinking tea and watching the container ships leaving the harbor. She joked that she would like to party with a tanned sailor, as she sailed to you, in America." He chuckles, "Mum. Hey?"

"I sent her a plane ticket," Jordan almost whispers.

"She said flying is for the rich and the angels."

"A trip at sea would have killed her-"

Silence.

Jordan forces another smile as he continues. "She read all your books- Your novels and she boasted about your achievements."

"I was so absorbed in my writing- The publisher puts a lot of pressure on me during marketing periods. I didn't realize Mum was fading so fast." Jordan whispers an excuse.

David reaches for Jordan's hand. "She believed that she was going to be healed by her church," he scoffs, "she wants us to scatter her ashes into the ocean. We'll have the ceremony on the pier."

JORDAN'S RELIEF IS almost palpable when they arrive at the Port Elizabeth hotel.

Maybe I should tuck and roll, she amuses herself.

Brian gets out first to unpack her bags. Jordan sits, paralyzed with insecurity. She would have preferred it if Brian remained in the car. David tries to comfort her. "Relax, sleep and shake the jet lag."

Now I have to face him again. Fuck!

When Brian opens her door, she hesitates. Brian is the first to break the atmosphere, "I have ordered you a nice rental so that you can drive around as you wish." David joins in, "I have to be in court tomorrow morning, but we'll braai at Brian's place later in the afternoon, when you are well rested?" Brian dips and peers into the car. "I would love to have you," he says with a smile.

Jordan pretends to be hesitant at first, but the handsome man's spark and her brother's boyish excitement, make it hard to resist.

"I know you are burning to go back, but this week-end is ours. Okay?" David adds.

She nods, kisses David on the cheek and alights, where she comes face to face with Brian.

"Sorry, I was talking through my neck," she apologizes.

Brian sounds serious when he says, "That's okay, everybody conceals their true emotions behind trivial sarcasm, or behind the canvas of a make-up mask."

"Meaning?"

"I'm just fucking with you."

Jordan returns a sheepish grin. "I don't hide, Mister Profiler man. I acted like an insensitive jerk. I don't know why. Thank you for the invitation. I'll let you know soonest."

They stay still, like it's a moment to say something more, before the hotel porter arrives to load her luggage onto a trolley. "We'll share a bottle of Cab and catch up. I like the accent, by the way." Brian winks.

"Is the team captain asking little ol' me out for wine?" She stabs back. A homeless man, draped in a soiled South African flag, shuffles closer. Jordan swoops in behind Brian's back, holding onto his shirt. The man signals that he is hungry.

Jordan catches her breath and glances at the beggar, takes a few dollars from her bag and hands it to Brian. Brian, in turn, hands it over to the grateful man and points to the Hotel. "You can exchange the dollars for Rands at the hotel."

The man staggers off, leaving a fetid fragrance behind. Brian looks at Jordan in appreciation, his voice a semi-sarcastic tone. "Look at you. You've done a good thing. The tin woman still has a heart."

Jordan kisses Brian on the cheek and follows the porter.

Where the building's pillars cast a shadow, close to the entrance of the hotel, a tall man is smoking a cigarette. He exhales the fumes, stamps out the butt and precedes inside, just as the guys leave the parking area.

-SEVEN-

†

Tonight's sunset is a master piece in watercolor wash. Saturated cloud palettes of apricot, fuchsia and teal, blend seamlessly on God's canvas. The ocean lies hushed in admiration. Across the harbor, Stewart is violently sodomizing Georgina Zweni.

His callused hands are on the back of her neck, pushing her head deeper into the coarse sand of the isolated memorial park. Georgina blasts up chromatic debris in an effort to survive, while Stewart is focused on reaching orgasm. He fails. Upset, he lets go of the whore. He zips up.

The heavy-set Georgina is livid. Her Cape-colored accent shines through. "Fuck man, what is wrong with you! I said straight fuck, not in my *hol*. I nearly died! Fuck it, man!"

Stewart doesn't respond. He slumps forward, out of breath, sweating. Taking money from his pocket, he flings it at Georgina. The slut crawls to get her panties, buried in the sand, then she picks up the crumpled notes, checks them and flies off into another tantrum, "Hey! You owe me double, I said a straight fuck! Not anal."

Stewart ignores her and sits down to roll a joint, but Georgina isn't done bitching, not when it comes to payment. She moves in front of him, underwear in hand. "Jou ma se poes! You owe me fifty more!"

In an instant, Stewart flies into a blinding rage. He leaps up and knocks her down with a merciless head-butt to her face. Her nose and lip split open. A crimson tide streams down her mouth and chin, mixing blood with panic sweat.

Georgina struggles to retain consciousness.

"God help!" is all she can manage.

"Yes. Call him."

"Jesus. Jesus. Jesus."

"Now I'm god," he laughs. "And I'm your only Jesus now."

She attempts to scream, but no sound can emanate from her because Stewart is hunched over the female, with her panties cinched around her neck.

"And I'll take your suffering away."

He is holding on tight with his right hand, with his left he loosens his pants and drops them to the ground. He grabs Georgina by her Afro, twisting her on her stomach, pushing her face into the sand. She has to force her neck sideways, to breathe. Stewart forces himself into her anal cavity and rapes her with bruising, savage thrusts.

Georgina now frantically fights for survival, her body going into spasm, as Stewart uses both hands to control the ligature around her neck. He rolls her on her back.

Pulling tighter, he repeatedly slams ferociously into her. Georgina claws her nails deeper into her neck to get a hold of the ligature. She recognizes her ultimate demise approaching. Slowly she yields, running out of oxygen and options. Then she surrenders to the call of the aphotic zone. Her face turns from brown to magenta. She jerks involuntarily, her lips and tongue bloating due to the slow venous compression, eyes bulging, jutting out of their sockets. This grim transformation sends Stewart into a frantic climax.

He viciously jolts over backward as he reaches orgasm, riding rodeo, like a cowboy taming the mare, he tugs onto the ligature. He faces the sky and remains almost motionless as he ejaculates. He howls like an animal!

They both go limp.

When he eventually stands up and pulls up his pants, he looks around in a bemused state of mind. He circles the dead woman twice.

Her contorted face is clogged with sand. Blood congealed. Breasts exposed. He stares at her dark nipples, swearing under his breath.

"Whore! So where is Jesus, hey?"

From his pocket, he retrieves an Okapi pocket knife and flicks the blade open. He stands over her, waiting patiently for his heart rate to settle.

Then he goes to town. His frenzy escalates as he repeatedly hammers the blade into her abdomen; Quick, violent strokes. There is no arterial spray because there is no heartbeat. He falls back, spent, panting like a dog. Blood thumping in his head, breath rasping through his chest, while he studies his creation. Rectus abdominis on a patch of brown. His eyes scan her breasts down to her black patch. It's a pity that they both missed the splendid sunset.

-EIGHT-

†

Jordan is awakened by a high-pitched scream! Startled, she sits up in bed.

Was it mine? Oh, it's only a car's tires screeching.

Relieved, she falls back, trying to regain control of her senses. The late afternoon sun, slanting through her window, brings a sense of comfort. She hears someone talking in the hallway, gets up and moves swiftly towards the door. She listens intently, pressing her ear against the door. Silence.

Quietly, she unlocks the door, grips the handle and swings it open.

Nothing. Nobody!

She sighs, jumps on the bed, only to find one of her hair extensions between the pillows. Irritated, she opens her laptop and checks her unopened mail, bank statements and book sales.

Admin done.

She flips through an album of black-and-white pictures taken of her mother. Her favorite portrait is a hand-painted image of Mum in her wedding dress. She attempts to find strength and wisdom in her mother's eyes. Jordan presses the photo to her chest and sobs. "I miss your love."

Then she places the pictures back in her bag and pours a coffee. Dark. Unsweetened. Which she drinks while staring out the window.

She's just in time to capture the sun's steadily ascending face, as it peeks through stacked blinds of brushed alabaster stratus clouds. The citrus sky forms a perfect backdrop. Jordan sips the beverage before another flood of emotion threatens to overwhelm her.

From her open luggage, she dons a designer white tracksuit and branded sneakers. She pushes her ponytail through the back of a matching cap, grabs a dark red rose from a vase and sets off.

AS JORDAN STROLLS DOWN the long pale concrete pier, she notices that the sun is suspended directly in front of her. *Walking towards a new light.*

Her only comrade along the way is an elderly fisherman in a worn green jersey. He tilts his hat as she passes.

Yesteryear he was considered a gentleman, today he may be labeled as a player.

She smiles to herself.

I must remember this line, it's gold.

Jordan reaches the solitude of the jetty's end.

Only me and the open sea.

She gazes into the turquoise pool, in an attempt to peer beyond the mesmerizing surface and perhaps find a submerged gem on the ocean floor. The cool swell lures her to lean over the railing, teasing her to take a plunge into the playful waves. From this height, the waters almost seem harmless. Even magnetizing.

Instead, Jordan drops the flower into the water where it stays suspended on the surface for a moment before the swell frolics with the rose, tugging and rolling it, until it drowns. Jordan stretches her arms open wide and belts out a refrain from a Frank Sinatra song.

> "Then softer than a piper man,
> One day, it called to you,
> And I lost you, I lost you,
> To the summer wind"

Further down the pier a tall, dark figure of a man watches her perform. He discards his cigarette into the sea, then like a movie director, he forms a frame with his thumbs and index fingers and places her in the middle.

Jordan turns and is mortified to find herself at the center of the stranger's orientation. The intruder drops his hands. He peeks across his finger frame, grins and then strolls away, leaving Jordan mortified.

-NINE-

†

David bursts through the courtroom doors, followed closely by Sergeant Cheryl Peters. "David, calm down!"

"Fuck this!" David is oblivious to the skulk of councilors and the flock of respondents watching them, fixed in hushed amazement. "Three years of my life wasted! Lack of evidence? We had the fucking money from the vault in their van, Cheryl! They got away with this shit in Jo'burg and now, again!" He slams his hand against the wall.

Four African men, sharply dressed in business suits, approach the detectives and form a square around them. Iggi is dark, bald, with a heavy Nigerian accent. He gets right up into David's face, while the others close Cheryl out of the conversation.

"The dragon and his angels waged war, and they were not strong enough, and there was no longer a place found for them in heaven." Iggi's black serpent eyes spit racist venom. He can hardly control his hatred and voice level as he hisses in David's ear. "Whitey! I told you- Angels fall, they burn out but I don't. Fokkol!"

David is ready to flatten the ogre. "Get out of my face, Iggi!"

"You should have taken the money, Boertjie. What would have been in your pocket? A million? More? Now another cadre has your million. And me – I still have plenty left! And how much you got? Africa- gives- a fuck."

David shoves Iggi back. They circle each other like prize fighters. Iggi sneers, displaying a golden grill. He raises his fists, triumphant. Apollo Creed, right before the titles roll.

David wants a sequel. "This is not the end. I'll be coming for you. You can't buy everyone." He is an agitated wasp, he raises his voice to ensure that Iggi's pack hears his following statement. "The thirteen million you stole won't keep you out of jail forever." The reaction amongst the cackle of hyenas is immediate.

"Stop talking piss!" Iggi seethes, "the charge sheet says six. You confiscated six million." Iggi casts a look at his plurality. "You heard the judge?"

"Then seven didn't make it to court?" David acts stupefied. "Honest citizen like yourself; your word carries a lot of weight, I'm sure,"

Iggi pushes past his men to get to David. He stabs a finger in David's face. "Fuck you. You need to learn the love and respect for money or you are going to die alone, pissing yourself in a government hospital. I'll be surrounded by sluts and nurses, maybe one on my face, when the tunnel of light comes!" Iggi whispers.

David grabs Iggi by the back of his shaven head, pulls him close and sends the message down his ear canal. "I'll be the one to bring you that bright fucking light, fucking soon."

Iggi struggles to pull away from David's vice grip. When he lets go, Iggi stumbles back a few meters, before recovering his dignity and pose.

"You owe me six bar. And I aim to collect," he smirks and leaves, boxing the air like a title holder, with his cackle draping behind him. David points a finger gun at him and pulls the trigger. "Boom, mother fucker."

Cheryl pushes his hand down. "It's okay."

David slumps down in despair, "No- He's right. I have fuck all. The honest die with fuck all. I need a drink."

"Hey, hey- We all struggle to pay bills. We are called the middle class."

"Fuck that! The judiciary is infected, corrupt politicians prance around in their Armani suits, dragging their snobbish whores on shopping sprees while cops and soldiers get paid chicken feed to clean up the streets around their security estates."

David's phone rings. He collects himself. "Detective Worth- Where? Okay. We are on our way." Collected, he looks towards Cheryl. "They found the body of a boy in the Target ravine"

-TEN-

†

Detective Colonel Claassen meets David and Cheryl, as they arrive on the scene. He opens David's door. "How did it go in court?"

David can't hide his disappointment and neither can Claassen, when he responds to the Colonel's query. "They went Scot-free Colonel. Not even a citation for dressing like a moppet."

Claassen, with hands on his hips, glances at Cheryl. He shakes his head. Cheryl knows, her saying anything, won't change a thing. They proceed towards Brian at the crime scene where CSI, dressed in flimsy white plastic overalls, are collecting every conceivable sample while documenting the macro scene on both Betacam and photographs.

Brian kneels to point out the leather belt wrapped around the throat of the decomposed corpse. The photographer captures the detail for him. The body of the 14-year-old boy lies obscured inside a marshy trench. It is obvious that some locals use this area to dump household waste. So too was the boy, discarded, like trash. Murdered and left to decompose under bubble wrap, chicken bones and bleached cardboard.

David opens his file to share a photo of a different victim with the team. "This is Monte Fiko. He was killed back in 1990." He shows a second image. "A year later we found a John Doe. If you look at these two images and compare them to our scene. They might be linked to the same killer."

Brian agrees. "This boy is badly decomposed." CSI adds to that. "I don't think we have a chance of lifting DNA here." Brian turns to Cheryl. "What is your assessment?"

"Cause of death without a coroner's report? Ligature strangulation. He was killed here. And again there's the roll of newspaper stuck in the anus. Signature- A necrophiliac. He comes back to them." Cheryl proclaims. "Victim- A colored boy, so our killer is probably a colored man."

Brian is impressed with the sergeant's observation. "The boy knew the killer. No vehicle, thus a low-income earner. Did he lure the boy here?"

"Probably with cash or with a KFC burger," Cheryl answers. "It has become a street commodity with which to buy teenage sex. It's known as KFC sex."

Brian smiles." I'll make a profiler of you yet. Anal rape is a sadistic act; the killer was victimized at about the same age as his victims. Maybe a bed-wetter beyond the age of twelve or an arsonist. We better be paying attention, because our man enjoys killing boys and he is gaining momentum."

-ELEVEN-

†

Stewart stands silhouetted against the descending orb, his coat flapping frantically against his body. His face is flushed, frenetic hair dancing around his head. Planted and stooped over like a willow, battling to stay vertical against the relentless gusts sweeping across the hilltop, he stirs the broth on the boil. He had to dig a hole into the rocky hill with his hands to ensure the flames stay contained.

Little Wuané shields herself amongst the honey-bush, knees drawn under her chin and her top stretched over her skinny legs. She rocks herself to and fro.

"And are you cold?" Stewart draws a thick green tarpaulin closer and covers her with it. "You want some soup?" He picks up a tin cup and points to the pot, "It's chicken," he yells, but the words still don't reach her. Wuané shivers, she stares at him with a vacant expression. He puts her cup down on the paint-splattered tarp. "And you'll be hungry later and I'll keep it here. It's going to rain tonight, I think-" He shades his eyes to find the skyline beyond the hotel.

"And so- Is he still hitting your Mum? And you?" Stewart's mind starts to drift, as he serves to incite himself by rapidly pacing around the fire, his body jerking in a slant, resembling an ancient's war dance.

"And I promise you, if that Michael touches you- I am going to take you away from here and maybe I can find a cave to hide you and you can stay with me, forever. God knows, that man is fucking evil."

He halts. Wuané's eyes are fixated on her feet, she doesn't react. She doesn't betray any emotions. A shadow seems to draw across Stewart's face. "And does he touch you? You know- And has he taken his pee-pee out?" He takes a step toward his daughter. "And Wuané, it's okay. You must tell me and not your mother. She won't stop him and you must tell me. Okay?"

Stewart drops down and crawls up to the fearful little girl. He is in total silhouette, all she sees is the outline of a plump, hairy head.

"Listen girl, I want to see something! Take off your panties," he whispers in a gruff tone.

Wuané doesn't stir.

"Wuané! Take off your panties. I won't hurt you. Fuck it!"

He loosens her grip when she desperately tries to hold onto her clothing. Her resistance is futile. She relents.

"Let me see. Lie back!" She does as she is ordered to do.

He crawls up between her legs and inspects her genitalia, not knowing what proof he seeks. He licks his pudgy finger and slowly inserts the soiled digit inside the whimpering girl. Then he sits upright, panting. He starts snarling and growling like a dog.

-TWELVE-

†

A terrified two-year-old Stewart, scampers underneath the kitchen table. The length of jump rope tied around the toddler's chafed neck restrains his movement. He is contained within the radius of the line's length. Doep has full control of the other end, curtailing the child, who is snapping and snarling like a rabid animal.

"Voetsek! Don't you growl at me!" He kicks at the boy. "Go lie down. Voetsek!"

The man-child scurries off towards a secure corner, where a frightened fox terrier has already taken cover, tail tucked deep underneath his quivering body.

The boy sees the bloated, wheezing man flop down hard on a kitchen chair. The seat's stainless-steel piping flares open, the worn plastic stoppers thrust scuff marks into the linoleum, and the seat's screws strain to keep it together.

Doep stares at him with charcoal eyes for what feels like an eternity. Once more, Doep wraps the rope around his fat, freckled hand, and slowly drags the terrified boy closer and closer to him, while he unzips his stained brown corduroys.

DOEP'S UGLY MUG STEADILY morphs into the fat face of a fornicating Deacon. He is sodomizing a boy. The skinny eight-year-old is bent over a solid oak desk, forcefully held down by the man's straight arm, gripping him tight behind his neck.

Gritting his teeth, tears streaking down his dirt-streaked cheeks, his focus is on a colorful jar of jelly beans on the table, mere inches away. The boy is soundless. Eyes wide in desperate prayer. Parched lips pleading for deliverance. "Please Jesus, please Jesus, help me. I beg you God. Stop him. Please Jesus-"

The boy's pleas go unresolved. He is delivered unto the indomitable malice of his tormentor. The clergyman grunts aloud. That's the sound he makes when he climaxes. The violator keeps the child pegged as he collects his faculties. Ashamed, he turns away from his deed, while strapping on his belt. Unable to face neither his sin nor his seed spilled on the ground.

"I won't tell anyone that you smoked, okay?" he puffs, wiping his forehead with his tie. Stewart remains motionless, his arms stretched wide. A shameful boy, sacrificed upon a wooden block. Taking the Deacon's sins upon himself.

STEWART JERKS UPRIGHT, his eyes flutter open. It takes a moment for him to realize that he is neither in the deacon's house, nor under his own shelter. He is inside the sturdy walls of an old fort. He lies down again, feeling safe, holding onto the boy next to him, secure in the knowledge that tonight he's not alone.

-THIRTEEN-

†

Brian adds rocks to their whiskey, while Jordan scouts the room. "Open plan kitchen and living area with big TV, a typical bachelor's pad," she jokes. Not even the rugged boxing bag, dangling from the porch roof, feels out of place. "What can I say, I'm a boy," he smiles.

Instinctively she rearranges the décor in her mind's eye to add an overall feminine touch and ambiance to the place.

Men hate that.

She scans through his ensemble of rugby and cricket memorabilia. There are several photos of Brian in his sports kits, brandishing an award or trophy and in most of the pictures, his proud father stands next to him.

On a side table his police ID, Beretta 9mm, and a Rossi .38 Special are placed next to a hand radio, ready for quick response. She resists the urge to touch the firearms.

Brian moves around the suspended *Everlast* boxing bag with ease to check on the fire. "We are almost ready to braai," he announces, "and your brother is late."

Jordan appreciates the romantic atmosphere of a room illuminated by candles, in the knowledge that it always compliments her white business attire.

On the coffee table sits a large jar of jelly beans, aesthetically sorted into the pattern of the South African flag. Layers of black, blue, yellow, white, red, and green sweets, stacked to the brim. Brian joins Jordan on the couch with two whiskey tumblers and hands her one. She motions in the direction of the beans. "My favorite writing partners."

"I bought it like that. I just liked the look of it. I have an attraction to Jelly Beans."

"Oh my god! I am so relieved," she laughs, "for a moment there I thought that you arranged them in layers yourself."

Brian hands her a dry smile. Another appeal of his, is a woman who can dish out a sarcastic roasting.

"Fun sweets, but I read somewhere that an overdose leads to anxiety," Jordan continues. "You've fixed the place up. It looks nice!"

Brian frowns. "Nice? Just nice?"

Jordan chuckles as she stands up. "For a man, yes, nice. For a woman- Too much gray. You need a splash of color in here."

Brian just smiles. "Well, it has been what? About five, or six years? And you have only been in here twice? Now you're revamping the place, already."

"I know you guys hate it when we disrupt your pads with feminine flavors," she retorts, "I'll definitely keep the photos of you and your dad. He was an amazing man and I admire that."

"He was my rock."

Jordan steps out onto the porch. Brian observes her lines and movements for a moment, before following her outside. From the porch, Jordan has an unobstructed view down to the beach, where a full moon plays peekaboo with the clouds above the vast expanse. She can hear the ocean as it's hushing itself to sleep. Brian leans on the railing, watching Jordan rather than the view. "So many people have palisade fencing now," she remarks.

"We have an affliction of self-righteous vermin who keep the honest citizens hostage in their mortgaged homes. It's mostly due to political greed and rising inequality."

"That's why I left," she whispers.

"The accent is now part of you. Like a Charlize," Brian teases. Playfully, Jordan punches his arm. "I work hard at being the best. I enjoy my status, I must confess. I know I need a new challenge, but the fans enjoy my novels and the moola is good."

Brian touches her glass, before lifting his in a toast. "And you are brilliant at it. You deserve all the success and for making it big."

"You may have been part of my romantic inspiration without knowing it," she teases, "but you never noticed the middle-class girls from Algoapark."

Brian mimics Jordan, pouting his lips and raising his eyebrows, "You rugby players, always with the booby blondes," he squeaks, in his best rendition of a teenage girl.

Jordan laughs from her gut and falls into Brian. Then she pulls back. Brian clears his throat to retrieve his normal voice, "My dad had money, not me. I was a teenage boy with insecurities aplenty."

Jordan is still wiping her eyes. "You never talk about your mum?"

Brian doesn't react. Jordan hands Brian her drink, steps back and punches the *Everlast* bag with the skill and acumen of a pro. She is amused by the surprised expression clocking on Brian's dial. "Wow!" He exclaims.

"I can shoot as well," she giggles.

"The question is, will you," Brian says.

She strides into the house and collects the snub nose revolver lying next to Brian's service pistol. "Why two guns?"

"Back-up insurance," Brian jokes, "hopefully, I'll never have to claim."

She pops open the revolver's loaded cylinder, spins it and with the flick of her wrist, she shuts the chamber back into position. Grinning, she returns the firearm, takes her glass back and moves towards the sofa. "One of the advantages of research. I get lost in the mad-cap escapades that a great book brings. The scent of a new book is my line of cocaine. I can't be recovered."

"That's how I remember you- Socializing with your nose in a book."

"I love adventure or getting lost in the mad-cap escapades that a great novel brings. The odor of a new book is my line of cocaine. I can't be recovered." Jordan sits down. "Besides, I feel awkward at social events. Cinderella to the extreme. Getting dressed up just to be ignored- I get lost in my addiction. In the escape where I would get noticed- Famous and successful." Brian still watches her attentively. There is a slight pause before he responds in a mild tone. "Well, for what it's worth. I had a slight crush on you."

"Only slight," Jordan flirts. "Tell me something- Something secret about yourself."

Brian joins her on the couch. "Okay. I'll confess to a secret. Then it's your turn to share?"

"Oh, goodie! Confession time." She takes a long sip while Brian puts his drink down and collects himself before starting. "My mother didn't love me. For a reason- nobody knows. Not even herself- So, I became ill," Brian pauses. "I developed a condition-"

"So you developed body dysmorphia," Jordan interrupts in a display of discernment. "I read about it when I did research a while back."

Brian is pleasantly surprised. "I hated my body. I even removed the mirror from my room. At 13 it became my obsession to pack on muscle." Jordan leans in closer.

Suddenly the hallway light turns on, spoiling the mood and the rhythm.

Jordan states the obvious. "The power is back on. Yeah, SA!"

"I never went to the social events either," he gets up to turn them off again. "I felt indifferent, I stayed at home, watched every detective movie ever and read true crime novels!" Jordan reaches out and touches his hand.

"Dad spent a lot of money on sports and clothes for me, but it never filled the void. I felt unloved."

Jordan squeezes his hand. "It's astonishing how incredibly important our primary caregiver's love is and how adversely it can affect our adult psyche," she says.

They exchange tender gazes. "This must be the longest conversation we've ever had," she smiles.

"I guess I was destined to be a psychologist, I am better at listening than at sharing."

They stay in the moment before Brian leans in.

"I'm separated-" Jordan feels the inexplicable need to confess. Brian pulls back. "Do you love him? Does he still love you?"

Uncomfortable pause.

She shakes her head. "I think he loves the idea of me, the limelight and the social status. However, whatever I felt for him, has been crushed under his bulldozer of insults." She takes another sip or two before she tries to lighten the mood. "Tonight I realized that I don't know you, Brian. Maybe if you didn't hang out with so many dicks back then-"

Cheryl barely knocks as she casually enters through the front door, adapts according to the mood, and chalks up a joke. "And a dick is no fun if it's propelled by an even bigger dick!" Then she gestures an apology and continues to retrieve a whiskey tumbler.

Jordan is taken aback by the woman's surprise entrance. "And who is this gorgeous woman with such lovely hair?"

Cheryl holds out a hand. "I'm Cheryl. Sorry, I didn't mean to interrupt, but it would have felt a lot more pervy if I just snuck back after accidentally- eavesdropping."

Brian takes the glass from Cheryl's hand, breaks a Johnny Walker's seal and pours her a drink. "Voyeur. Where's David?"

"I lost my partner," Cheryl smiles, "How many cops can say that?"

"It's better than missing your period." Jordan delivers her gag and receives an "Amen!" from Cheryl.

"Jordan, this is Detective Sergeant Cheryl Peters of the Child Protection Unit. Cheryl, meet the lovely Jordan."

Brian hands Cheryl her Walker Black, as his phone rings.

"Hey man, where are you?" Brian excuses himself, steps onto the porch and closes the door. The women touch glasses and continue with light, introductory conversation.

"Tell me about yourself?" Jordan starts. "Oh! Like Brian said, I'm a cop at-"

"I mean what is it that you do there?"

"I work with abused children, broken homes but mostly runaways and street kids."

"And homicide? With David?"

"That's very noble. How is my brother doing?" Jordan inquires.

"Considering everything he juggles, I think he is doing well," Cheryl replies. Jordan scrutinizes her and Cheryl immediately recognizes that her answer is not to Jordan's satisfaction.

"Consider then, that I love and care deeply for my brother, the soul closest to me?"

Cheryl is taken in by Jordan's candor. "Your jab landed, lady," she grins and inhales. Her tone turns almost apologetic when she speaks again. "Let's see. A painful divorce, your Mum's sudden passing, not seeing his daughter as often-" Cheryl's voice starts to tremble involuntarily. Her blue eyes reflect vulnerability. "Rolling black-outs, fifty murders per day and we earn peanuts." Cheryl searches for a something to lean against and finds comfort on a leather chair's armrest. She lowers her voice. "He conceals inclinations towards addictions. David escapes via alcohol and gambling, to keep a dream alive, instead, he's living a reality of nightmares."

Jordan moves in and hugs her. "Thank you for your honesty."

"Almost every man I have ever been with, was abusive in some way. Mentally. Physically. And mostly towards themselves," Cheryl continues.

Jordan needs a moment to ponder the statement and steps away from Cheryl, breaking eye contact for a while. "Maybe it's because we feel damaged that you- We are drawn to people with broken wings. Nothing to fix, nothing to love." Jordan says.

"Do you think that we should discard the broken in order to survive rather?"

"Meaning?"

"I have seen women walk away from something real because they are petrified of being vulnerable again."

"Or maybe we build up an intolerance for bullshit when you've been fed every line from the Truelove playbook?" Jordan says. Cheryl shrugs. "I hear you. But these two guys are cut from a different cloth.

"I'm listening."

"Anyone could be forgiven for expecting these men to be tough, macho or disconnected, like most people in this job." Cheryl says, moving in front of Jordan. "They are excited to have you here. Both of them. Do you hear me?"

Brian returns to a silent room. "Everything okay?" he frowns. Cheryl slides down into the chair. "Dandy."

"David says he isn't feeling too well-" Brian starts to lie, but Jordan interrupts. "I know."

Brian sighs. "Of course you do. He is still at the casino. He said that he is going to take a taxi home to sleep it off."

Cheryl gets up, grabs her car keys. "I'll go get my partner." Then, in a USA military-style voice she shouts out, "I've got your six, Captain!" Cheryl salutes the air. "See you later guys! Don't touch my drink." They laugh at her antics, as she dances out the doorway. "I like her." Jordan smiles before she hands Brian her glass and switches to her Vivien Leigh impression: "Now, decanter some of your finest scarlet wine, as I need to seek out the old water closet."

-FOURTEEN-

†

Stewart tries in vain, to steady his scarred hands, when he fires up another hand-rolled joint. The fag's peculiar incandescence illuminates his vulnerable state. He wipes the wet from beneath his leaky eye.

Profound lines manifest across his stark expression. The grooves plowed into his face, are carved out by relived traumatic experiences. Childhood trauma! The damage that can't be cured, not in one lifetime nor one generation. It becomes DNA.

With damp eyes he watches the population spill onto the promenade below. It's their regime of amusement, called nightlife. For the homeless, it's bedtime.

Bedtime is when Stewart is hyper-vigilant, it's when his stomach starts to churn and burn. He is caught in a fight, freeze or flight mode. He hisses all manner of ungodly phrases underneath his rasped breath, as he collects and slings stones at the blissful citizens.

Not unlike all his needs, the cast rocks fall far short of the objective, they land where the dried grass is caked with his vomit and nobody's life budged. Spent, Stewart plops down on an abrasive boulder jutting out of the dirt, he finishes the quart of beer before he notices the fire's embers displaying a last few tired blinks.

He scampers to find fodder and rubbish to get it burning again and stacks up a few logs to ensure that it keeps the site illuminated.

Sleep won't come easy, but *they* will if darkness is not kept at bay. *They* come calling on stygian nights. Predators and prey alike, circling just beyond the rim of the fire's gleam. Only their haunting stares are visible, bloodshot eyes, judging his sins.

Stewart crawls under the coarse plastic sheet, in front of his daughter. Her eyes are closed. He reaches back and drags her fragile body tight against his back. "Goodnight Wuané."

No response. Dark clouds start painting the moon black.

-FIFTEEN-

†

J ordan studies every portrait on the walls of the hallway.

Again, my curiosity exceeds my need to pee!

It's mostly a curious montage of darling family photos interrupted by amateur paintings, where a celebrated artwork was printed on canvas and the recreational artist attempted to paint-by-color over the original piece. She smiles.

Brian's dad.

In passing Brian's study, she notices a framed portrait of Brian and his girlfriend on the desk. She peeks inside only to find a second photo of Brian, David and herself in high school. The amateur image of the boys flexing their biceps, is slightly out of focus. In the background is rosy-cheeked Jordan, a ponytail perched on top of her titled head, resembling a cockatiel trying to learn a new phrase while she is slurping up melted ice cream from the side of a cone.

Her lips are covered in a sticky mess and there's a vanilla smudge on the tip of her freckled nose.

The little shit! I'll roast him for this.

She smiles and enters the room, tip-toeing like the Pink Panther. Case files on the desk catches her eye. She leans forward to check.

What is in there? This is wrong.

She flips the file open to reveal ghastly photos of a strangled, bloated woman, mottled patches, bulging eyes, lividity, rigor mortis, maggots, garrote, dirt and death!

The sudden impact of the images propels Jordan out the door, down the hall towards the bathroom, almost knocking frames from the walls.

When she reaches the bathroom, she is able to suck in and release a deep breath.

Fuck!

Hyperventilating, she grabs hold of the white marble basin, to stabilize her spiraling psyche. Her drained reflection in the mirror, shocks her back to reality.

Why did you open the file?

Grabbing onto the basin, she slides down on the closed toilet seat.

How is it possible for the mind to capture so much detail at a million frames per second?

Jordan has the instinctual need to splash cold water on her face, even stripping down and jumping through a shower in an attempt to cleanse her being.

Water would be a dead give-away, her calculated sense informs her. The water running across her palms is soothing.

Compose yourself and put on a star performance, you've had to fake worse.

She empties her bladder, washes her hands, checks her hair, straightens out her white suit and struts back down the hallway.

-SIXTEEN-

†

B rian baptizes a flayed beef fillet in a rich, red, "left-over-wine" marinade, before gently laying it down on the sizzling grill. The aromas of a South African "braai" fill the dark heavens, as the blend of spiced vapors and hardwood charcoal plume into the firmament, much like an old testament burnt offering.

Jordan swigs her wine down and refills her glass, without Brian noticing. He is deeply focused on perfecting their meal. He slices and dices the colorful ingredients required for a Greek salad, before adding a handful of cashews and drizzling his secret sauce over the nutritious dish.

This allows Jordan that slight window of opportunity to regain her composure before she engages him in small talk.

"Your house is filled with beautiful memories. I hope you preserved the jovial, mirthful Mr. Harper as well?"

"It took a lot of therapy to make me jovial and to stop abusing myself."

They both chuckle as Brian sheepishly tries to recover from the faux pas, but then lets it go. He turns the meat.

Jordan takes a seat and another sip of her Cabernet, before speaking. "What is it like, to be a profiler? With all of the- with all these cases and corpses? I mean, once I start a book, the characters live with me. They possess my thoughts until the novel is finished."

Brian fixes his gaze on the smoldering coals, as if to find the correct response in the fire, before he asks, "Do you remember reading *The Rime of the Ancient Mariner* at school?"

"Yes. Wow! Coleridge right? "And listens like a three year's child","
she says, quoting from the poem. Jordan follows him as he steps into
the lounge, retrieves an aged bundle from the large wooden bookshelf,
opens it and hands it to Jordan to read.

"The Wedding-Guest sat on a stone.
He cannot choose but hear;
and thus spoke on that ancient man,
The bright-eyed Mariner."

She levels the book. "So how does this pertain to you, or your job?"

Brian remembers the meat on the grill, sprints out and rescues their
steak. "Ah, perfect. Let's eat." Jordan takes her seat at the dining table
and watches him in amusement. "Does this happen often? Don't worry.
Lots of chefs have no talent at all." He laughs as he joins her with a
heated Pyrex bowl containing the treasured fillet. "If I had a dollar-"
Brian slices the steak into portions, while Jordan dishes up the salads
for them.

He tops up their wine and drops down next to her at the table's
corner.

"The poem holds this universal truism for serial profilers. Just like
the guest, we feel the need to understand why the Mariner would slay
an innocent albatross and just like the Mariner, the killer displays a
need to find catharsis for his deeds, by re-telling his story."

"Wow, Mr. Harper, that is deep and poetic. I'll have to study the
poem again."

"We are working two cases. Someone is targeting homeless boys
while another killer is preying on prostitutes, both in the same city, at
the same time."

Jordan sighs, "God, that's not for me. But it seems that we all have
this morbid curiosity when it comes to serial homicide?"

"I think that serial homicide, offers society a glimpse into the next
level of depravity. By being a witness to it, we also find absolution for

our primal urges. But the more the curiosity, the more the depravity we witness."

Brian nods in agreement. "That's the conflict that consumes the souls of the people involved in a case. You sink, by untested levels, into the abyss. And then, to find your way back safely to the harbor."

"That's when the wind dies down." Jordan grinds black pepper over her steak. On the side of her plate, she adds copious amounts of course salt. The traditional South African way: You dab a thin slice of meat in salt, no sauces.

"I'll never be able to drag myself from the abyss with my faculties intact."

"Just like the Mariner," Brian responds, "nobody does. Serial homicide is not for everyone."

-SEVENTEEN-

†

Stewart battles to haul the naked and contused body of Katriena Claasens across the thick beach sand. His stumpy fingers clamp around the ex-prostitute's ankles, as he drags her bulky frame towards a bantam wall with bright graffiti on it.

"And fuck it, you are too fat." He pants and drops her feet to catch his breath. His eyes have adjusted to the surrounding darkness, but the ocean remains hidden in an ink void.

Almost there.

He grunts, squats, grabs her by the pods again and pulls her towards their destination, only a few meters away, cursing at the knolls of sand accumulating in her crotch as he plows the shore.

Eventually, they complete the journey, where he plops down next to her behind the wall, out of breath. A yellow plastic bag protrudes from her mouth and a garrote is wound around her throat, burrowing into her flesh. The absence of livor mortis points to a fresh kill and the deep, bleeding claw marks and facial petechiae indicate that the whore's swan song was a violent score.

With trembling fingers, Stewart prepares a fag. He grabs a pinch of marijuana from his pocket, adds some powdered Mandrax, drenches the paper with saliva and then skillfully rolls the joint into a paper sarcophagus between his thick, scruffy fingers. He spits out an unwanted shard of grass.

As he strikes up a match, the gaudy graffiti on the wall becomes legible. It reads: THOU SHALT NOT STEAL!

-EIGHTEEN-

†

"When did you learn to box?" Brian asks Jordan as he joins her on the porch. Jordan tries to deflect an answer and responds with a playful, "So girls can't kick ass?"

Brian plays along. "In movies maybe. Come on! This is what I do. I observe. And you know how to punch like a trained fighter. You've got the eye of the tiger."

"I do? God I love that movie." She knows that she needs to disclose more info to satisfy the profiler.

"I picked it up, at a local gym. We must go shooting, then you'll be impressed." She says, employing wine to moisten her lips. Brian studies her for a moment before turning his gaze to the fading embers. He speaks softly. "Did he hurt you?"

"Never again-" It's barely audible. Her eyes turn towards the fire and they both stare into the faltering coals, waiting for the uneasy moment to pass. Then Jordan changes the subject. "Aporophobia and Peniaphobia. I am fearful of poverty."

At first, Brian is at a loss. Jordan organizes her thoughts as he catches up. "I get anxious about losing everything. Poverty spawns domestic violence, crime and uneducated adults, which leads to chronic, long-lasting poverty."

"I share your anxiety. We are gradually losing our healthy middle class-" Brian responds.

There is a knock at the door. David and Cheryl enter the room to interrupt the conversation.

"It's all about mindset." David is under the influence of jovial spirits. "The mindset of the 'here and now', not on the consequences of the behavior."

Jordan likes to see her brother this way. "You're in a good mood?"

David flops down in a chair. "I feel like a winner!"

Cheryl goes directly for the coffee maker and fills two mugs, hands one to David. "Sometimes the odds are just stacked too high," she says.

Jordan nods. "Maybe. I still believe that anyone can escape their past and reset their life."

"Or make enough money to buy the stacked-up odds." David quips. He notices the *Rime of the Ancient Mariner,* jumps up, grabs the book and plops down again. "Money makes the world go round and the boobs bigger!" They laugh at his antics. He holds the book up. "But you can't rehabilitate the tortured souls. Fucked for life!"

There is a slight lull before Jordan speaks again. "Is it macabre that you, or-most of us, find serial homicide fascinating?"

"Maybe it's because we have this primeval fear of stalking beasts," Brian responds. "I think that our ancestors couldn't deal with such an atrocity in a village."

Then to the amusement of the trio, Brian reaches for an hourglass to serve as a Memento Mori, strikes a thespian pose and delivers his prologue. "Many households alike, with no dignity. In fair antiquity, where we lay our scene."

The "audience" reacts in wonderment as Hamlet delivers his lines. "Alas! Just imagine, if you may, poor Yorick, a serial killer terrorizing the land. The tribe would discover the mutilated remains of a maiden and blame it on a ghoulish beast. Not for a single moment, would they believe that one of their own, is stalking their women folk in such a depraving manner."

Brian hunches over as the witch of Macbeth takes center stage. "So foul a fair murder I have not seen," he crackles, "where myths of monsters and demons sprout its roots in superstition, as superstition begets religion."

Brian takes a deep bow and his antics are met with laughter and applause. Cheryl is the first to speak. "So Little Red Riding Hood, was more at risk of being violated by her lustful uncle, than being attacked by a wolf in the woods?"

Brian returns the prop and takes hold of his glass. "As soon as you understand the monster behind the myth, the story unravels. Today we study the psychological imprint he presents on the scene and then we decipher the slayer's fantasy."

"Are they born killers, or do you attribute it to a life of abuse?" Jordan asks before Brian responds. "Neglect. The neglect of a baby by its primary caregiver, is the most inhumane punishment you can inflict on an infant. For an adult, it's isolation. Genetics, combined with personality, early childhood trauma and the environment they live in, all drive serial homicide behavior."

Cheryl sees Jordan's growing interest. She teases, "You should write your next book on these two guys and what they do. The detective and the profiler." David jumps in. "Call it- Harper's Worth or A Worthy Harper."

"Yeah? It sounds enticing-" Jordan says. She then turns to Brian. "You better educate me first. I do proper research."

"You are welcome to work here."

David is about to levitate. "Are you serious? I would enjoy having my sister around to observe what we do! See? Now you've got two books to write!"

Brian touches her shoulder. "Serious risk to your mental faculties- remember that."

Jordan takes the whiskey bottle, fills up Brian's glass and plays a provocative look. "Into the abyss I say! Africa is not for pussies!" They all hoist their glasses and *cheers!*

"Salute!" David shouts, chugging his drink down like it's a shot. Brian meets Jordan's gaze and she replies with a sly smile. "I know- Serial homicide is not for everyone."

-NINETEEN-

†

From Stewart's vantage point on the rocks, he sees the morning sun, attached like a halo around the timid frame of Harry Baker. The boy comes frolicking along the shoreline, prancing in and out of the surf, raising his knees high to navigate the undulating swells.

The nimbus reminds Stewart of the baby Jesus in the stained glass windows of the Cathedral Church of St Mary's.

No, even more like the mosaic of a crucified Messiah at St. Augustine's Cathedral.

Since childhood, he groveled and confessed before both divinities on umpteen occasions, without response or intervention. By now he has come to the supposition that no one cares, neither an adult virgin nor an innocent infant turned pharisee, even less so, a distant deity.

Fantasizing about being a cricket icon, Harry swings a pale plastic container around like a bat and strikes at the airborne spume. On these scorching weekends, Harry sneaks away from his chore of buying milk, to take a quick dip in the ocean or just to stroll down King's beach, to cool down as the thin layers of waves lap across his legs.

Not even the regular beatings he receives prevent him from hiking to the pier for a dip. Without fail, the skinny teen would touch the compassionate heart of a passing Samaritan, and Harry would find himself on the back of a truck. Hitching a ride is just another way of commuting for the poor. This morning he had to be up early because Grandma needs to bake Mealie bread and Mosbolletjies but *someone* finished the milk last night. Harry bats another ball for a six before he notices a perched Stewart and without whoop or motion, approaches him.

Harry knows better than to holler at the mariner. He finds a spot on the rocks below Stewart, then slants a look in his direction. Stewart continues whittling a piece of driftwood, ignoring the boy. For a while, they stare at a freight ship leaving the harbor.

Then Stewart folds away his blade, exchanges the knife for a nipped joint and lights up. He siphons the tobacco smoke through his lungs in five long hauls before offering the last puff to Harry. The boy inhales and hands the joint back to Stewart who declines with a wave. Harry flicks the fragment into the rocks. He feels free to engage. "Boetie, have you heard anything from Wuané?"

Stewart dons the most unsavory expression with ease.

Harry alters the conversation. "I've got a girlfriend now. Her name is Belinda."

"Belinda? And is she pretty?" Stewart assumes a grin of the greatest self-satisfaction. "And living on a boat house?"

Harry's expression twists in proper puzzlement; he doesn't know the hit song. "She is beautiful. But she doesn't live in a boat house?"

Stewart smiles. "And you are too young to know the song. And do you fuck?"

"No!" Harry protests, "I am a virgin and she is too. I don't know what to do."

"And how old are you now?" Stewart interrupts.

"Almost fifteen. But she is almost sixteen. You must help me."

Stewart scoffs, "And I have been fucking from when I was younger! All the time."

A nervous giggle escapes Harry. In the same instance that he glances up, he catches the recognizable voice of his classmate, waving and calling out to him. He jumps up and directs his friend to leave. "Loop hier! I am talking to Boetie. I'll come now-now!"

Stewart joins in when the boy hesitates to heed the warning. "Hey, voetsek!" He throws a rock at the teenager and the boy scampers back a safe distance. Stewart gets up and casts a few more stones at the retreating target. "Let's go."

"I have to catch a ride back. Ouma is waiting for the milk." Harry protests.

"Then go wank your friend." Stewart is adamant enough to spark doubt in the boy's mind. "And we can't talk here and that bean will tell- Fuck 'em." Stewart pushes his hands into his pockets and steps off the rocks with Harry following in close proximity.

"Let's go lie low." Stewart suggests, his feigned features, heavy set. Harry's friend continues to follow them but soon abandons the futile pursuit. *It's no use.* His calls kite across the Indian Ocean.

-TWENTY-

†

The quartet of mourners stand in stark contrast, against both, the bleak Shark Rock Pier runway and the lucent sapphire sky. By simple coincidence, Jordan and Brian are dressed in matching monochrome gray suits, a detail which didn't escape Jordan's attention earlier.

Now, in her trembling hands, she holds the little box containing Mum's ashes, as she recites the eulogy she indited on the plane. "There are many things that a woman should never have to suffer; abuse, the forever departure of a child and a notion of abandonment."

Her eyes move from David to the teal waters. "A vibrant woman working towards a civil society, you were often rewarded with hostile slogans, profound violence and terminal-" The surge of emotion rising in her voice flows through the group.

"Mommy, you sacrificed your body for love, you yielded your dreams for love, you surrendered your soul for the sacred love of a mother."

Jordan forces a brave facade. She then stops, holds her breath, averts her eyes and bites her quivering lip. But her effort to regain control of her spiraling emotions elicits the polar effect in Cheryl, who buries her sobs in David's chest. In support, Brian places his hands on Jordan's arms and an unrestrained, spiritual sorrow flows through Jordan's eyes. "Mum, you taught us to live in the moment, to never wait for tomorrow, but here we are, tomorrow has arrived and the rest of our tomorrows will transpire without you." Jordan weeps. "We return you, our trove of glimmering gems, back to your beloved sea."

Jordan drops the burgundy box onto the swaying waters. The others follow with red roses. The Indian ocean plays with her gift for a while, before she conceals the treasure under her teal garment, forever.

-TWENTY-ONE-

†

The bartender serves Jordan her second glass of Cabernet.

She winks in appreciation, then she leaves her lipstick marks on the rim of the glass while she scans the venue.

Way too early to be drinking.

Apart from their quartet, the hotel bar is almost devoid of guests. At the end of the counter, Cheryl is comforting David and finishing her cigarette.

Brian returns from the gents. As he sits down, Jordan takes another sip. "Do you believe in the afterlife?"

Brian turns on his seat and ponders before responding. "Afterlife, like in a religious sense?"

"Like in, I hope to God I don't have to start all over again, in another life. I would prefer heaven."

"I believe in reincarnation, or I did back when I was Alexander Hamilton," David jokes, as he and Cheryl shuffle closer. "A glow stick has a brighter future than you." Jordan roasts. Cheryl is more serious with her input. "I have seen too many evil fucking humans than to believe in a mythical red devil."

"I would like to believe that kindness and morality stem from our choices, not from the religion that you are born into.," Brian adds, "you choose to be either moral or evil."

"Free will," David interrupts, to which Cheryl responds, "Apparently, free will gets you into hell. We see so many victims, who must have called upon a god in their time of anguish, all in vain."

Jordan raises her glass slightly. "Represent, sister! If you only live once, you take more responsibility and live out loud?"

Brian touches her hand. "If we love our children more than we love our possessions, the world won't need a messiah."

While Jordan ponders the idea, David breaks into song. He grabs Cheryl's hand and leads her away for a dance.

"I believe the children are our future, teach them well and let them lead the way..."

Jordan and Brian join in singing, raising their glasses in a salute! "To Mum! I love you!" David shouts, followed by Jordan. "For every sacrifice Mum! I hope we make you proud."

Brian's cell phone rings. He steps away from the others before answering the call. "Colonel? No, it's okay, the service is over. I understand- I can go- Prince Alfred Park? I am on my way."

Brian indicates to David that he must be on his way. "Another woman has been found in Prince Alfred Park. I have to go." He turns to Jordan. "Please excuse me."

Instinctively, Cheryl grabs her phone and keys before Jordan protests. "Wait- Can I go with you? I want to go-"

Brian looks at a shrugging David, hesitates, then nods. "I'll check with Colonel Claassen. Cheryl, can Jordan ride with you?"

Cheryl approves. "Sure."

"Wow. I am shaking!" Jordan exclaims. She looks up at Brian. "Don't stress professor profile, I am only here for research. I won't get involved and I'll still write you in as the protagonist, the hero."

Brian renders a dry smirk, he hands his keys to David and starts dialing. As the two men leave, Jordan turns to Cheryl. "Do I seem crazy?" Cheryl winks at her. "The best person to ask, is yourself."

-TWENTY-TWO-

†

As they turn into Park Drive, Jordan can't ignore the irony as they pass a decrepit crowd squatting amongst human waste, outside the gates of the cemetery, which is sandwiched between the prestige lawn of the tennis club and an art gallery.

Dead center of town.

A few meters down Park Drive they enter the Prince Alfred Park grounds. Cheryl stops her vehicle, nods at Jordan and they alight in unison. As they pass the Prince Alfred's Guard Memorial, Jordan's memories come flooding back. "I have spent many a fun day here, now there's this hostile energy," she remarks with a hint of melancholy in her voice.

The Memorial, which is situated on top of Port Elizabeth's second oldest water reservoir, commemorates the British men who lost their lives during the campaigns of the Empire's *"Building thrust in Africa."* Britain established power in Africa through brutal force, which was often bloody and merciless.

The women are intercepted at the base of the statue, by a uniformed officer. Cheryl produces her police ID and proceeds to fire up a cigarette.

The officer relays a message as formally as he was instructed. "They will confirm when you are sanctioned to attend the scene." Cheryl finds a seat to bask her legs and savor her cigarette. Jordan circles the memorial, running her hand across a lion's head motif and down the brocaded names of the fallen. Although it's Victorian in style, the monument is not monochromatic, like most of its type. It's been painted using colors from a limited palette: Olive green, muted maroon and khaki so it blends in well with the surrounding African landscape.

Far removed from yesteryear's brazen soldier in the defensive stance, posted on top of the Memorial with bayonet at the ready, today the only steel piercing flesh, is a needle stabbing a vein.

With the toe of her boot, Jordan prods the discarded debris of a hypodermic needle, toward a brimming waste bin. Evidence of an overnight flight to obscurity.

Brian arrives to escort them toward a clump of trees. "You have been cleared to attend the crime scene. Please do not touch anything, no matter how trivial it may seem. If you cannot stand the sight or get upset, Cheryl will escort you back to the car," he says.

"Thanks. I will be okay," Jordan replies. Cheryl pats her on the back. In their stride, they pass a few uniformed officers enjoying a lunch break and two thin mortuary men cracking a joke while waiting to stack their "*Meat van.*"

"The indignity of homicide and suicide," Jordan mumbles to Cheryl, who is already donning a set of opaque white latex gloves, which she blows up like balloons before she stretches them over her hands. Then she strays off, leaving Jordan in Brian's care.

It's only once they reach a cluster of trees, that reality truly sets in. The undeniable pungent stench of rotting flesh hits home first, landing right on the crop of her stomach. It sends Jordan reeling. She covers her nose with her palm and flares her nostrils in an attempt to repel the stench.

The next punch lands in the shape of a sprawled, nude cadaver. It takes a brief moment for Jordan to decipher the details of the horrific scene unfolding before her.

Is this a human being?

Millions of maggots infest the decaying meat and flies swarm the bleary CSI team in their white coats. A pair of young policemen record the process on video and stills.

Jordan instantly recognizes that familiar, overpowering response starting to take hold. She turns away from the mutilated corpse, grabs onto the support of the closest tree and hyperventilates. Brian hands Jordan a bandana from his pocket to cover her nose. "How are you doing?"

Jordan raises a hand to request a moment, perishes her thoughts and turns to face the maimed body. "I am okay," she whispers through the cloth, fumbles to open up her memo pad and nods for Brian to continue.

CSI finishes up and allows the detectives and camera crew to step in as they unfold a black body bag. David signals to the eager videographer to capture Brian's analysis on tape.

"Okay, we have the mutilated body of a 42-year-old female, Georgina Zweni, known to be a local prostitute. Sodomized, it seems. But, it may have been consensual." As he speaks, Brian's gaze oscillates between Jordan and the camera lens.

A piece of Jordan's hair extensions drops onto her shoulder. Brian walks out of shot, collects it off her jacket and hands it to Jordan. "Are you sure you want to continue?"

She puts it in her pocket. "I am okay," she smiles before Brian returns to the corpse to continue.

"Cause of death seems to be ligature strangulation," he says, pointing at the gouging garrote, with his pen, "but then our killer went ballistic. She was stabbed repeatedly around the navel area and he sexually assaulted her with a sharp instrument. He inserted the blade into her vagina and sliced upwards. He removed her nipples with either the blade or with his teeth."

"Holy shit! Why?" The remark escapes Jordan, even catching herself off guard. She places her hand back over her mouth "Sorry."

David smiles. "It's what we call "overkill". His sexual fantasy is escalating." Brian follows up. "It's all about exerting control over his victim."

Cheryl approaches, carrying a black plastic bag which she opens for Brian to peek into. "I may have found the rest of our victim's clothing-dumped in a fish pond."

"Our man is learning," Brian says.

"By watching us?" David mutters to Jordan. He takes a moment to scan the curious crowd, held at bay by flimsy chevron tape and indolent cops. He calls out to the photographer and sends him off to capture images of the assemblage.

Brian continues his presentation with the videographer. "In all, we counted at least 20 stab wounds and a cluster of cuts next to her navel. We refer to it as picquerism."

Cheryl turns to Jordan. "The knife is a metaphorical substitute for his penis; the manifestation of a boy who fixated during the oral phase of his development. Freud"

Jordan swats at a pesky fly and pens down a note. "Meaning?"

"He's an oral sadist. The biting of her breasts points to a subconscious attempt for breast milk. It's like a baby biting his mother if he feels he is not getting enough milk."

Brian delivers another remark into camera. "That fixation has made our guy over-sensitive to rejection- Freud."

Jordan's eyes rolled up to the corpse's face. All the evil that had transpired was still there, eternally encapsulated in her glazed dead eyes.

-TWENTY-THREE-

†

Concealed inside his soiled green hoodie, a squinting Stewart tries to hide his identity by blending in amongst the snoopy spectators. He can barely contain his excitement. What he wouldn't give to be able to walk up to the cops and discuss the case with them!

He is condemned to listen to these- Meerkats share their absurd insights and fake news snippets as he meanders amongst them. Some of the citizens call out to the officers for clarity, some joke, most of them are appalled. Stewart feels himself getting an erection.

Then his eyes land upon the most beautiful blond woman in the gray suit. He halts. Transfixed. The sounds of the crowd drown away.

She admires my work.

He pushes his way to the front of the crowd and grabs hold of the chevron tape. The *"click" of* a DSLR jerks him out from under the spell. Realizing that the police photographer may have already captured him on film, Stewart rips the hoodie's string to close it up before he hastily disappears to the back of the mob, cursing the cops for trying to trap him.

He waits for the photographer and the rage to depart before he escapes the crowd. With his hand sliding along the police tape, he follows the boundary of the crime scene. He stops to take a long, last look at Jordan before he departs toward the cemetery.

-TWENTY-FOUR-

✝

The metallic cavity of the *"Meat Van"* stands ajar in anticipation of transporting its passenger to the morgue. There, the Forensic Pathology Laboratory will perform an autopsy before issuing a death certificate and a full report. If nobody claims the remains, it becomes a government concern and she would receive a pauper's burial.

Jordan moves out of odor range. From this perspective, she feels more like a spectator of a crime drama and manages to find humor in the macabre scene. The mortuary men are perched on their battered trolley, similar to a couple of vultures patiently awaiting their turn.

The CSI squad unzips the rubberized shroud, before positioning a man at the corpse's feet and another at the shoulders.

This is going to be grim.

In the movement of transferring the cadaver into the bag, a soup of fluids seeps out from almost every orifice. Squirming maggots drop off her like animated confetti, while red dust and mud clings to the buttocks of the body. Jordan swings around to avert her eyes.

Fuck, that's enough for the day.

Brian's calm and reassuring voice turns Jordan's attention back to his investigation analysis. Cheryl is conducting an on-camera interview with him. "Indications are that he also fixated during the anal phase which is an element of sadism and control over the victim." he says.

"Too bizarre," is all that Jordan can manage.

"He sodomizes the women as it degrades and punish them.

Our killer may have been raped as a boy." With that, Brian concludes his final analysis. The cameraman drops the hefty Betacam from his fatigued shoulder and joins his partner at their vehicle.

A peculiar hush descends upon the setting. Jordan slumps forward, anticipating the sound of the body bag's zip closing up. When the rasping tone finally pierces her ears, her hair follicles jump on end. She tries to rationalize her response, but there's none to be found.

Once they leave the trees, she finds her voice returning. "I'll have to read up on Freud. Both the men you are after, are disturbed to the extreme," Jordan says, focusing her eyes on the monument. Brian takes Jordan's arm and guides her towards his car. "He was probably abandoned at birth or before the age of two. Our boy, is venting his Oedipal anger at mother figures, for not being there to protect him."

"Okay, that is all still Freud? How is it possible to have no empathy and no sense of guilt?"

"All serial killers fixate during the latency phase, then in one or more of the other phases," Brian responds then hugs her. "You did well."

Jordan slumps down against his vehicle, masking her mania with a laugh. "I need to soak in a hot bath." Brian opens her door. "Am I allowed one last question? How the hell do you catch a killer?" she says, getting in.

Brian holds the door. "Normally, with a rope- Enough rope."

Jordan scoffs. "Around his hands or his neck?"

"To catch a serial killer means becoming obsessed with the case, the victims and the killer himself." He says.

"Beware that, when fighting monsters, you yourself do not become a monster- for when you gaze long into the abyss. The abyss gazes also into you," she replies.

"Nietzsche?" Brian checks.

Jordan smiles. "Did Nietzsche construe with the profiler or the monster?" Brian winks and closes her door.

-TWENTY-FIVE-

†

In his chapped hands, Stewart fidgets with a strand of red polyester rope, tying and untying sailors' knots. He senses the presence of Wuané behind him, her eyes burning into the back of his skull.

She is not in a happy place.

"Wuané, I have to protect you from this world." His words are scarcely audible, most of them are blown off by the cool evening breeze. "And you are lucky- And you have a father. I don't even know mine."

He slowly turns around to face the little girl, who sits curled up, holding her legs. Her eyes are dewy. "And I will be here every day, you hear me? Every day." She doesn't react and just stares at Stewart. He pulls a plastic tarpaulin closer and lies down in preparation for sleep. He holds the cover open and invites her in. "Come lie here with me and I can see you are cold."

Wuané crawls in and they spoon under the grating plastic sheet. "And I want to find an Island like Peter Pan- And we'll sneak onto the boat." As the sunlight finally dies off, he hums an Afrikaans lullaby "Siembamba, Mamma se kindjie-"

67

-TWENTY-SIX-

†

David sits hunched over, behind a bunker built from cardboard manilla case dockets, stacked up on top of his government-issued desk. More bundles of files litter the moderate office. The paper tower stacked behind his door prevents it from opening all the way.

Cheryl reads his nameplate aloud in the hallway before entering with coffee. "Detective D. Worth. You are bright and early in your little Jenga box- Or have you not been home since yesterday?"

Before he can answer her, his phone rings. "Homicide, Captain Worth. Yes. Yes! That is great news. Thank you." He hangs up. "I love our lab rats, especially when they tell me it's looking positive on the boy at the ravine."

Cheryl hands David his coffee and a missing persons report. It states that Harry Baker is a missing individual. "I have just filed a 55A with the mother of Harry Baker. I have a hunch you may want to interview her as well."

David takes a cautious sip of the scorching black brew. "Thanks." He removes a pile of dockets from his desk and stacks them on top of another slanting heap. "I should be a fucking chess champion. Bring her in." Cheryl leans out of the doorway and returns with a thin, middle-aged, colored woman. She brings with her the irrefutable odor of *Lifeboy* with her. They sit down after exchanging pleasantries.

"Please call me David." He scans her statement inside the file. "Misses Baker, you say that your son has now been missing for two days?

"Yes. Harry went to the shops and from there he was supposed to go to my mother's house in Missionvale," she starts.

"And you live in-?" David interjects, still scanning the affidavit. "Ah- Algoa Park. Sorry, continue."

"Yes. But that one is naughty. He always gets a lift to go swimming."

David interrupts again. "I used to do that back in the day too. Where does he swim?" Ellen thinks before responding. "I think he meets his friends at that beach at the Red Lion." She breaks down and shudders uncontrollably. "I didn't miss him until this morning, when my mother came to me and told me he was not there."

Cheryl hesitates then places her hands on the mother's drooped shoulders. "It's fine, Ellen. I have given out a report, as well as a description of Harry, to all patrol units. We will find your boy."

Ellen unfolds a crumpled tissue from her jersey's cuff and mops her tears. David confirms more details. "And your mother, I presume she doesn't have a phone,?"

"No, she doesn't."

"Anything else? Anything you can think of? Friends that he might be staying with?"

"Harry's friend said he saw him with Stewart at the beach."

"Stewart?" David asks.

"Stewart Wilken. Boetie. I worked for his family, then he was my boyfriend. I kicked him out because he smokes himself moff- Stupid. He mixes dagga and Mandrax- then he becomes violent."

Cheryl sounds concerned. "Did he hurt you and Harry?"

"All men hit. He is kind to Harry and the other kids."

"His daughter is the Wuané Wilken girl who went missing in 1996," Cheryl informs David.

"Do you think the kids are with Stewart?" David asks.

"I don't know. The children are always talking to him."

"He is charged with molesting two brothers." Cheryl interrupts, her tone betraying her annoyance. "I checked," she says, waving a copy of the charge sheet. "He didn't show up for court on Wednesday."

David reads her, loud and clear. "Ellen, where can we find Stewart?"

"Most of the time, he is in the Missionvale shebeens. He is homeless."

"Does he work?"

"He works on the fishing boats."

David concludes the interview. "Thank you. The sergeant has taken down your statement and there should be a warrant out for him soon." Ellen departs with a simple, "Goodbye." David collects his jacket and keys. "Let's go pub hopping for a hobo."

-TWENTY-SEVEN-

†

J ordan is absorbed in a crisp copy of Robert Keppel's' "*Signature Killers*", when Brian places a cup of steaming mocha on the side table. Jordan shoots him a "Thanks!" before turning to her PowerBook for further reference material. Brian chortles. "What?" Jordan asks, bemused.

"Nothing," he smirks, knowing that a disappearing pencil, like the one slipping in between the couch pillows, is Jordan's bane. Soon he'll be treated to another quick aria of rhythmic profanity, when the author goes into the hapless exploration of her implement.

Even though he experiences these performances once or twice a day, he still finds them amusing. If he didn't, he would inform her every time he spotted the stylus about to engage in a bout of "Where's that fucking Wally?"

Over the past week, Brian has been witness to a thousand spectacle adjustments, note-taking in the shape of undecipherable hieroglyphs and of course, her ferocious appetite for reading through a strong-room of online data.

He schedules the much-needed and compulsory strolls along the promenade, Q and A's on the pier, as well as an impromptu picnic, which went down exactly as he planned, because she "*loves a surprise*." So the distraction of a pencil missing in action is his sappy way of enjoying her presence in his home.

-TWENTY-EIGHT-

†

Inside a New Brighton shebeen, sweaty cleaners sweep up the expectations and debris from the previous night's bash.

Brown quart bottles of beer, stand half-empty on top of plastic tables. Semi-smoked cigarettes, some pasted with lipstick, are crammed into cups and ashtrays. "Everything in this life is half empty," David simpers. "Everything, but the ashtrays."

Shebeen is a South African word meaning "informal drinking den". The chairs and tables are made from cheap Chinese plastic. Some still remain overturned on the unpolished stone floor. The dull tin roof seals in the aroma of fatty ash emanating from a smoldering fireplace, blended with a hint of dried beer and body odor. True to the shebeen spirit, music blasts from giant battered speakers fixed crudely to the walls.

David screams at the disinterested owner, in an attempt to be heard. The photo of Stewart that he holds up, doesn't elicit a response other than a shrug.

David turns to the personnel for scraps of information, then returns to his vehicle with nothing more than the smell of disappointment clinging to him.

Cheryl stomps her cigarette out. "So? What life-changing epiphany did you experience in there?" David scoffs, leans on the roof of the car and peels off his shades for dramatic effect. "We don't hunt to kill. We hunt the killers, who hunt to kill."

"Oh that's deep, Mariana," she roasts him. "Can you see the Titanic down there?"

"Don't be a screen door on a submarine." David retorts. Cheryl hits back. "Your ambition outweighs your skills. "

They share a speedy grin. "Where to now, Captain Smith?" Cheryl jokes, slipping in behind the wheel.

"Let's check out the Walmer shebeen close to the airport." Cheryl gives David a quizzical look.

"You must have the same sense of direction as Columbus. Just go, I'll point out the way," he laughs.

Before driving off she rips him a last one. "You look easy to draw."

-TWENTY-NINE-

†

Jordan draws the gray blinds to shield her PowerBook's display from the morning sun's glare, when Brian enters with two steaming mugs. "I'm drinking too much coffee," she protests. "I need to drink more water."

"You can't, fish fuck in it."

"Ha, ha. If genius skips a generation, your kids will be brilliant."

"Your suit matches my blinds."

"I've seen salad better dressed than you," she grins. "I must find space for you in my luggage," she hits back, "you'll make such an amazing PA."

"You can't afford me, honey," he smirks, clunks down his mug and pushes an oversized mobile board, displaying the crime scene photographs of three homicides, to the center of the room.

Jordan is focused on completing her roasting. "Who said anything about pay? Just follow my instructions like a good-"

"I only follow instructions when I'm naked."

"Oh? Then strip and listen to me," she says, folding her arms.

"Many a true word is spoken in jest my dear, many a jest-"

Jordan grumps. "Okay Bill Jester, where were we?"

Brian returns her smile and then motions her attention to the board. "Georgina Zweni."

"Oh yes. Can we go back to the first victim?"

Brian nods. "Victim one is Virginia Gysman. Strangled at the Dagbreek Primary School. Anal penetration. October of 1990."

Jordan shows a thumbs-up before he continues. "Victim number two is Mercia Papenfus, also a prostitute in St. George's Park. January 1991."

"Prostitutes are easily accessible and explicitly connected to sex." Jordan confirms her notes.

Brian continues, "And now, Georgina Zweni, strangled near Prince Alfred's Park. Sodomized. He then proceeded to sexually assault her with a blade."

"Prostitutes flaunt their sex and these "whores" need to be punished?" Jordan ventures. Brian takes a seat on top of her desk. "Well done. Anal rape is classified as sadistic-"

"Sadists relish in the pain of their victims, so they torture their victims in an elaborate fashion or signature," Jordan completes the sentence. "And yet, this guy does not torture the victim, he kills very quickly. But he still gets his erotic pleasure from the kill. Remember, I have a very graphic mind. I see in pictures."

Brian leaps up. "Yes. And so?" Jordan responds with a lot of confidence. "He most certainly had a caregiver who neglected and humiliated him."

"And if you had to render a diagnosis?" Brian pushes.

"He doesn't trust or respect anyone."

-THIRTY-

†

BOKSBURG, SOUTH AFRICA, 1968.
The two-year-old Stewart is hunched in the corner of the dark kitchen, feeding from a dog bowl. He scoops the food akin to a monkey using its paw, then he grabs the bowl with both hands and licks the last morsel from the rim.

He is acquainted with the grim sounds emanating from the under-lit living room. A bloated, farting and winded old man's cursing, as he gasps for air. But what terrifies him the most, is when the terrier's intermittent yelps stop and all that he hears is the radio playing lovely, innocent, British hits and a sales jingle proclaiming Sunlight soap's superior cleansing power. Both, are in stark contrast to the soiled scene of bestiality playing itself out, on the man's decrepit velvet couch.

When Doep eventually tosses the dog away, it instantly scampers outside. Even the animal feels sinful. The boy instinctively knows what is about to follow. Doep's bloated frame appears in the doorway at the end of the narrow hallway, where he battles to find his balance.

No pants, just a T-shirt. A fucked-up version of *The Poo*. The nauseating odor of brandy and urine follows. As he drops down on a laminated kitchen chair, his legs spread and a small, semi-erect phallus dangling between fat, hairy thighs greets the child. Doep spills some of his drink and slurps it up from the table. "Come." He orders.

Stewart remains frozen, seeing only the man's lower body.

"Come here!" He barks. Stewart crawls towards Doep.

"Good Boy." The boy stops between his knees.

"Come on! Lick."

-THIRTY-ONE-

†

PORT ELIZABETH, SOUTH AFRICA, 1997.
Jordan is still entertained by Brian's sizable profile board, where the host of evidence gathered, is intricately webbed. Red string serves to link crime scene photos to images of the deceased, while green constitutes additional vital info. The only thing that's missing, is a suspect to match their profile.

Pacing around while reciting the bullet points, is Jordan's way of ensuring that information sticks in her mind, so she struts, as Brian prods her with snippets of mental content. "He could not identify with a male figure-"

Jordan shoots him a quick glance before responding. "He was ridiculed by his peers, he felt isolated- Withdrawn."

Brian gives a reassuring nod.

"Killers mostly target a certain victim profile-"

"Very few killers target victims from the opposite race."

"So we are looking for a colored male, with low income and low self-esteem." Jordan stops pacing and turns to Brian. "Oh, wow! That certainly narrows it down!"

"In that moment, when he is placed in front of you, you'll recognize him by his signature, because his crimes are fueled by fantasies, central to his being. Now, talk to me about his fantasies."

Jordan ponders her retort before speaking. "He fantasized about revenge, about being in control. Fantasies find fertile soil in the isolated and inside the mind of the tortured souls."

-THIRTY-TWO-

†

David steps out onto the albescent sand surrounding the Walmer shebeen and with his arm, he waves the stale air away like a smoker. The female cooks started preparing supper in massive, steaming cast iron pots, over an open flame.

That's what it is all about. Chunks of meat, beer and pulsating ethnic beats.

A troop of teens collect at the curb and a barrel more wait to intercept David, to beg for pocket change. But crossing a single palm with plated nickel, has the propensity to ignite an urban brawl. David sambas a pathway through the kids for the sanctuary of the car. The jolly mob pursues them gleefully for another block, before dispersing.

An amused Cheryl ends her phone call. "The charges of molestation against Stewart, are in connection with two boys from his second marriage to Veronica Wilken. Veronica didn't lay the charges. It was brought by his in-laws, her parents."

"Ta-da! The plot thickens. Well, the guys inside that cute dwelling," David says pointing with his thumb over his shoulder, "suggested that we go look for him at the docks. He works on a skip called *New Dawn*. Call Brian and ask them to meet us there."

Cheryl starts dialing as she tries out her best pirate impression. "Aye, Aye, off to da boats Captain. Harrr!"

-THIRTY-THREE-

†

C heryl hands Jordan and Brian their security passes when they meet up at the safety-office gate. The men lead the way as they journey amongst the motley rows of stacked skips and boats. A concoction of machine oil vapors and fish guts, stir up a potent odor.

Jordan watches the squawking Kelp gulls hover on the wing above, where fishermen are unloading and cleaning the morning's catch. Discarded fish heads and red entrails are caught mid-air, by the agile birds. Like a hatful of city dwellers, these gulls have recognized that begging or stealing, is an effortless way to survive.

Jordan's group make intermittent stops to inquire about Stewart, as they encounter dock workers. A burly man points them towards a faded green skip where Stewart can be seen gutting fish bait on a makeshift table out on the dock.

Jordan gently takes hold of Brian's arm and they stop. She studies Stewart for a moment. In contrast to her expectations, he is a man of little stature. Shorter than average, stumpy arms. Nondescript really. The last kid to be chosen for sports.

A blissful Stewart, sharpens a worn knife on a whetstone, before flaying a snoek with surgical ability. He tosses the fish guts towards the water, a darting gull snatches the meal before it can hit the sea. The heads are chopped off for bait.

He puts the snoek in a crate filled with ice, before removing his cap and wiping his forehead with his bloody sleeve.

"Wait here. You'll be fine." Brian assures Jordan.

Cheryl takes the lead as the trio approach Stewart. "Stewart? Stewart Wilken? I am Sergeant Peters. This is Captain Worth. Can we talk?" Unperturbed, Stewart selects another knife and chops the head off a snoek. He avoids eye contact with Cheryl. He addresses David. "I am Stewart." Cheryl looks at David and scoffs.

"Stewart, we are looking for Harry Baker. Do you know him?" David asks.

"Yes. Why are you looking for him here?"

"When last did you see him?" David continues.

"Wednesday I think. And he was at- At the fucking beach- And to buy milk for his mum and we talked a bit and then he left."

"What did you do after he left?" Cheryl pushes.

Stewart studies Cheryl for a while before responding. "I went to my girlfriend's place and I fucked her- I've got a fat cock." Cheryl's expression remains poker.

"And Harry?" She demands. Stewart avoids further eye contact with her. He looks down and carries on working. "And he fucked off to his grandmother's. And they treat him like a dog- Always kicking the boy and he is a good kid and maybe he ran away and maybe he sleeps on the beach."

Cheryl is not done. "Stewart, do you know where your daughter, Wuané is?" Stewart drops his head and shoulders. He leans forward on the table for a while before slowly looking up at the detectives.

Then he notices Jordan standing on the pier. Stewart's demeanor switches from bleak to jocular, as he answers without hesitation "I think she hides away-"

Eventually, he breaks his gaze away from Jordan, to rant at Brian. "And because that fucker treated her like a fucking animal, man. And no food- He hates children- That step-father and he is a fucking pig!" Knife still in hand, arms hanging, he slowly approaches Brian, shaking. "She told me everything and I could not help her."

Brian takes a step back. "I am sorry. So who is your girlfriend? Where does she stay?"

Stewart shuffles a few steps closer. Brian notices that both Cheryl and David already have their hands on their holstered firearms. David speaks up "Stop right there." Stewart takes another step.

He is within striking distance from Brian when he stops. He looks past Brian's shoulder to see Jordan and then back at Brian again. "Sharon Mackenzie- And she stays close to Algoa Park but I don't know the name of the street and you can just ask anybody at that park and they will show you."

The conversation has run out. Doubtful glances are exchanged. Suddenly, Cheryl's cell phone emits a loud beep. Unsure, she throws David a glance. He nods to assure her that he's got the fisherman covered.

She reads and relays the message. "The court warrant hasn't been issued as yet." Stewart returns to his table and David waits for him to be at a safe distance, before speaking. "Stewart, we'll be in contact later so don't leave town." As Stewart reaches his table, he searches for Jordan again. Cheryl steps into his line of sight. "May your life be as pleasant as you are. Catch you later."

David touches Cheryl's shoulder. "Let's check out his alibi first. Patrol can bring him in on the court warrant and collect DNA."

"Creepy fart! What do you think?" Jordan asks and It's the first time that Jordan finds Brian's answer vague.

"We don't prosecute creepy." He adds more volume to his voice. "What else did you notice?"

David too realizes that Jordan had missed the cues. Brian, trying not to be offensive, wants her to see the present danger. "What else did you see?"

"What am I missing guys?"

Cheryl comes to her rescue. "Stewie's fucking obsessed with you!"

-THIRTY-FOUR-

†

In the midst of an energetic match of street rugby the air is filled with the distant sounds of laughter, the muffled thuds of the rugby ball, and the occasional honks of frustrated drivers. Street rugby is played with a dirty rugby ball in a stadium with invisible lines. The players vacate the dust-covered pitch whenever a car needs to pass through before they flow back in, just like the Red sea once did.

The girl squad, chin-wag and admire from the sidelines, while younger children are relegated to spectate from the curb for safety reasons.

"They say all social bonds of the underprivileged develop in the streets," Jordan murmurs as they park behind David's vehicle. Brian takes her trembling hand. "These bonds supersede any pledge that the privileged can ever make. Once you forged a friendship, you live and die by affiliation."

As they step out of the car, a lanky teenage girl, her head hidden beneath a stained, blue hoodie, approaches Jordan. The air suddenly thickens with tension. David the protective brother instinctively steps in between the girl and his sister. His eyes narrow, an object, ominously resembling the shape of a firearm, is tucked into the front pocket of her hoodie.

In this suspended moment, the streets bear witness to a collision of worlds, where the divide between the privileged and underprivileged is starkly defined.

The girl studies Jordan's classy outfit and shoes. Soon the estranged adults, are encircled by a gang of hooded teens, who conceal their hands under their clothing.

The girl gently pushes her hood back to reveal her beautiful green eyes and blond hair. Jordan catches her breath at the remarkable resemblance. This youngster is a spitting image of Jordan as an adolescent. The uncanny irony is not lost on anyone. Jordan is still looking for a consonant to start a sentence, when the girl asks Jordan. "Lanie, wil julle koop of kom julle naai?"

Jordan frowns, "What did you say?"

David translates. "She wants to know if we came here to buy contraband or sex."

"How old are you?" Jordan asks.

The girl is amused and counters with a gag. "We can sex you too?" Jordan scans the grinning, acned gang of immature jungle-fowl. "What do you sell?" Cheryl inquires. "Anything that pops."

David wants to move on. "Do you know a boy named Harry Baker?" Silence. Cheryl flashes her badge. They don't flinch. "We don't want to buy anything. We need to get Harry back. Is he your friend?"

"He is not affiliated. But I know who he is."

Jordan unwraps a blue banknote and holds it up. "Do you know where he is, or when last you saw him?" The girl shoots a tall, chubby boy a look, orders are barked and the crowd is dispersed, leaving the girl with an open palm in front of Jordan. Jordan pays the hundred Rand over. "They say he went with Boetie."

"Boetie?" Jordan asks.

"Boetie Boer- Stewart."

Jordan holds out a fifty. "And do you know Stewart?"

"We call him Boetie. He's cool." Jordan pays again.

David looks at Cheryl. "The teenagers seem to like him?" Then he addresses the girl. "Where does Sharon Mackenzie stay?" She points to the house across the street, David turns to the girl. "Have you eaten?

Are you hungry?" The girl doesn't speak but she escorts him to the gate where she bangs on a metal post with a rock. "Nobody." She scoffs.

David pushes his business card into the gate and they return to the vehicles. "Are you not worried that you tried to sell to the police?" He asks. "Die polieste kom naai mos ook hier." David translates. "The cops come here to fuck as well."

The girl launches herself across the car's bonnet and slides off on David's side just as he opens his door. Jordan and Brian move closer to follow the conversation.

"What's your name?" The girl enquirers. "David. And yours?" The girl leans up against the hood and nods. David gets in and opens his window to listen to her. She pops her head through the open slot. "Sharp, Lanie! Sharon works the night shift. She comes home early." She holds up a peace sign. David imitates her and she laughs. "Then I'll bring you proper food with me tomorrow. Is there anything else you need?"

The girl doesn't answer as she retracts her head. David hands her his business card. The girl recovers her hoodie, scans the card and looks up at David. "Sharp, Lanie David. Do you have kids? You should adopt us." David's voice trembles. "Where are you from? Your parents?" The girl moves away and holds up a peace sign. "My life is a mystery with no conclusion."

Then she swaggers away, leaving the adult quartet with unarticulated emotions.

-THIRTY-FIVE-

†

"The pigs came today- Looking for you. And it was 2 men and a bitch cop who looked at me like I owe her something. Bitch!" Stewart spits into the fire. "Eat your chicken, Wuané"

He paces frantically. "And there is another woman- And I think she is the one I had a dream about- She is the one who is going to find you. I know it."

He tugs at his hair and lets out a growl before falling into the dust next to Wuané. He crawls closer and places his head on her lap. "And I am going to find a hole so deep to hide you, that she will never find you."

-THIRTY-SIX-

†

The waiter clears the dishes. Brian sips cautiously at his steaming coffee, when Cheryl returns to the table, after her smoke break. Jordan reads through her notes on her computer, with David browsing over her shoulder. Playfully, Jordan pushes him away. "Why would he have a fascination with me? Things just don't add up."

Brian manages another sip. "I know! That fucks with me. He ticks a lot of the boxes, but if he is accused of molesting his step-sons, why are they still alive?"

"Maybe, he is a pedophile and not a killer?"

"But then, who is killing the boys?"

David plays with the salt and pepper shakers. "He went hard on Cheryl by going completely obscene. I so wanted to flatten him-"

Jordan gives him a compassionate touch. "So, where are we and what is the next move?"

Brian leans back and smiles. "Oh, the novelist wants to work."

Jordan clears her throat. "Gentlemen, I have changed my flight plans!"

Both guys are fly up. David hugs his sister tight, almost restricting her from completing her speech. "I spoke to my publisher and she is interested in both cases. If I don't take back proper research my publisher will put me in one of your case files."

Brian laughs, gets up and kisses Jordan on the forehead. She almost melts but fights to keep her composure. "Relax boys. The truth is- my priority is to work with Cheryl and to save- find Harry and Wuané. I truly believe that I can do it."

David's phone rings.

He answers. "Captain Worth." A female voice with a strong Capetonian accent speaks slowly. "Stewart did not take Harry." David puts the phone on speaker mode. "Who is this?" Jordan leans in to catch the conversation.

"The Angels of Six took them. Boetie didn't take the children. They keep the boys and girl in a house for sex and to harvest their organs," the female voice continues in a monotonous tone. "They have already sold those children."

David pulls out his notebook. "Do you know where this house is?"

The call is disconnected. It's okay. Cheryl knows where this infamous house is situated.

-THIRTY-SEVEN-

†

Two SWAT vehicles roll up to a dilapidated house, badly in need of paint and miracles. The lawn has gone to shit. Stuffed trash bins wait in vain for morning collection and somewhere a resolute dog barks in desperation at nothing.

A few streetlights spatter and barely illuminate the situation. Maybe, the dark township lane is an effort to conceal the shame of decades' lack of political will. However, it has the opposite effect. It exposes the consequences of greed and state plunder.

Burly officers assess the area and suit up for house penetration maneuvers. Jordan takes a deep breath before getting out. David briefs SWAT officers armed with MP-5 sub-machine guns. 10mm is the standard caliber of the special task force.

Cheryl helps Jordan fit a Kevlar vest. Brian interrupts. "It would be safer to stay in the car."

"I can't write a novel from the back seat of a car." Jordan snaps at him. Brian capitulates, then hands her a flashlight and a can of mace. Jordan start taking notes. Her fascination shifts to the snipers moving, hunched over in formation, to cover the house from every elevated angle. Anything that may present a clear and present danger wil present in their scopes.

Police serve and protect, they are not military. There is never the intention to take a life, nor do they intend to lose one. She writes.

SWAT stack up at the entrance with Derrick, Cheryl, Brian and Jordan lining up behind them. Brian wipes away the pearls of sweat from Jordan's brow. "Stay close behind me at all times. I want to feel your hand on my back or my belt."

To drum up courage, Jordan keeps her focus on the police insignia, on the front of the blue balaclavas covering the faces of the officers. She feels her stomach churn, her temples pulsating.

Fuck, how did I get here?

She tries to decipher this- this illogical reasoning. But the more she tries to rationalize her fear, the more it seems to take hold of her.

Suddenly, the police illuminate the house with an intensity that may only be seen again at the second coming.

Bang!

The flimsy front door gives way and Jordan finds herself inside the living room. An overpowering stench violates her nostrils. The house reeks of body odors, stale urine, rotting food scraps and unwashed-everything!

The miasma of despair.

She pulls her bandana up to cover her nose. "Now I get why they wear balaclavas," she mumbles.

SWAT moves through the cramped and dirty spaces with intent, their gear clanging and scraping against the walls. Immigrants scatter and huddle in the corners as the team sweeps past them, guns at the ready.

Most of the aliens remain stagnant, disengaged from reality some are frozen, petrified, creating obstacles which slows the team down. The glare gushing through the windows, casts high-contrast shadows on the floor, making it nearly impossible for Jordan to differentiate between people and objects.

The sight of human beings, living in such deplorable conditions, is excruciating to watch. Families, five to a mattress. Gauzy, worn-out blankets. Terror etched on their faces, despair in their eyes. It's a stark reminder of the inequality and rampant poverty that exists in this country.

Coastal cities draw a steady stream of migrants and runaways, exacerbating the safety and law enforcement issues for police and the community. Smuggled in by road, by ship, in containers. It's a drove of illegal African women and children, who have ended up in this sty. Viva slavery. Viva!

David and Cheryl work in unison, moving meticulously from person to person, verifying identities under the scrutiny of a blinding torch beam.

The SWAT leader bark orders continually, pointing out potential threats, as they penetrate deeper into the maze.

Suddenly, the floodlights go out, leaving a carousel of blue strobes as the only source of illumination around Jordan.

"Fuck!" David curses,

Horrified, Jordan fumbles for her Maglite. It falls. Instinctively she drops to the floor, only to find herself face to face with a petrified boy, frantically clinging to his mother's chest. Down here, the pong of halitosis, sweat and transmittable diseases, stings her lungs. It's a potent concoction of abuse, hunger and abject hope.

Brian grabs her by the vest and jerks her off the floor, in the same instant she snatches her torch. Like a lightsaber hilt, it shoots out a white beam, slicing through the gloom. Brian shows her how to maneuver the heavy Maglite, by placing the barrel of the torch on her shoulder.

"Thanks."

Jordan shines the spotlight on the boy and his mother. There is a baby nursing on her breast. Jordan wants to speak, but Brian drags her down the hall where they step over more aliens, until they reach the main bedroom door.

It's locked.

The officers stack up.

Thud!

A solid kick near the locking mechanism and the door swings open to reveal an African man standing next to the bed, branding a machete. He is instantly trapped in the team's headlamps. A crimson laser stamps a tika dot between his eyebrows.

"Police! Put the weapon down." The SWAT leader orders.

The man does not react, but to Jordan's dread the commotion stirs up the female occupants on the bed and the children on the floor, like a scene from a zombie apocalypse flick they come to life, rising around the Rasta-man. Time seems to slow down.

Fuck. Fuck. Fuck.

"Put the machete down." The officer instructs again, firearm aimed at the target, who starts to tie his dreadlocks behind his head.

"*Someone is going to die!*

Brian pushes Jordan against the hallway wall and Cheryl joins to shield her. The house has gone as quiet as a tomb, in anticipation for the stand-off to play out.

A baby starts to whine. Jordan follows the sound with her torchlight. At the end of the corridor, a mother is pacifying her restless infant. She pulls out her flat breasts and props one into the baby's mouth. Another infant moves closer, squats, and latches onto her other breast to nurse, never taking his eyes off Jordan.

Jordan hears the machete clatter to the floor. SWAT moves in to overpower and restrain the man. Cheryl joins David to identify the occupants of the bedroom clan before withdrawing under the protection of the SWAT members. "Undocumented immigrants, but no Harry or Wuané," David confirms. "Let's go."

Brian moves past Jordan to take point for their extraction. The little boy stops feeding to look up at Jordan with moist brown eyes. His chubby lips ringed by a hoary sap.

A poster child for humanitarian aid.

"Wait!" Jordan says. Reaching for her pocket. "Why?" Brian inquires, grabbing her hand.

"I want to give her some money."

"Are you out of your mind? If you hand out money, they will trample us. We won't reach the fucking front door."

Brian's demeanor and words hit home, jerking her back to reality and the fetor of the decaying place. Jordan tenses up, and starts to shake uncontrollably. "Get me the fuck out of here!"

-THIRTY-EIGHT-

†

A topographical map of Port Elizabeth, lies sprawled across Brian's kitchen table. David adjusts a cluster of plastic pins as Cheryl confirms each locations with photos and detail of every victim. Brian follows their activity from the corner of the room, feet up, sipping coffee, and only lending input where it concerns his areas of expertise. Jordan watches from the porch, whiskey in hand, annoyed at another piece of hair extension falling out.

I am dying for a cigarette.

A habit she kicked years ago.

David starts. "Red pins, indicate where the boy's bodies were discovered. Blue, where the female victims were found. Green indicates the locations of all other homicides and violent crime anomalies we are excluding for now as it doesn't fit the MO or signatures."

David points to a red pin. "It appears that the first confirmed victim was murdered in February 1990. He was 15-year-old Monte Fiko-"

"Cellié High School. Thursday, 8 February 1990." Cheryl confirms. Strangled with the belt he removed from Monte's pants."

David gives her a quizzical look before continuing. "A street child of which, unfortunately, there are quite a number of in South Africa. The killer sodomized the boy at Cellié Secondary School in Sydenham and killed him there."

Jordan decides to shrug her crabby frame of mind and moves in to join the discussion. David points to a second red pin. "Then in October 1991. St Georges Park. John Doe, a 14-year-old street child. Male"

Jordan interjects to show that she's onboard. "And the blue pin at St Georges, is Mercia Papenfus. January '91."

Brian responds. "Correct."

"Have you considered the fact that your two killers might be working together? We had such a case in the U.S.A. known as the Hillside Stranglers." Jordan checks.

"Yes, we did," Brian responds. "The proximity of the crimes suggest that the killers are likely known to one another."

"We are keeping an open mind. That's why we profile more than one male, on all these cases." David replies before focusing on the map again.

"And of course, John Doe two, a teenager, sodomized and strangled at Target Kloof."

Brian adds, "The victim profiles, indicate that they may not be working together. At least, not in targeting the same victim type. Killer couples usually share a victim profile as well."

"The bodies were hidden, some with a rolled-up newspaper in their orifices." Cheryl says.

Jordan draws on stability from the last gulp of whiskey. "That is bizarre!"

"It prevents maggots from crawling into the orifice. He returns to the corpses. This man is a necrophile." David explains. Jordan frowns. "And the guy killing the women?"

"We suspect that he may be a necrophile as well," Brian answers. No proof as yet.

"So then, what is his signature? Sadism?" Jordan puts it to Brian.

"I suspect that our killer enjoys facing his victim's pain while raping, sodomizing and strangling them."

"Control?"

Brian nods.

"Some of the bodies were in a bad state of decomposition. We couldn't retrieve DNA," Cheryl states before Jordan interrupts. "We should have saved that woman and her children." She's got everyone's attention. David sighs. Jordan turns to pour another drink. "Sorry Cheryl, but I should have given that woman money- or helped in some way."

"I understand how you feel," Cheryl says.

Brian takes the bottle from Jordan and pours her the drink. "The three base motives are domination, manipulation and control," he says, adding ice before handing her the glass. "He feels inadequate, inferior, but when he kills, his victims are completely under his control."

Jordan takes a sip. Brian continues. "By being in control of another persons life, he feels as if he has control over his own life. A god complex."

Jordan withdraws to the lounge. "I need to go back and get them out of that house." Brian follows her. "And do what with them, Jordan? They need be deported home. Money alone, won't save them all."

"Enough money would. I believe I can save the mother and her two children."

"People save people. Only Ubuntu can change this continent." Cheryl says, and David responds to that. "Those in power grab the money meant to uplift the vulnerable. The tragedy is that Africans vote for politicians who don't build anything."

"Let's focus on finding Harry and Wuané." Brian says.

Jordan snaps, "It's not like you are saving anyone-"

Silence.

"I am- We are focused on finding them both."

Jordan moves back onto the porch to grab oxygen. David takes his car keys. "I have to go. It's an early morning for me. Alibi checking-" Cheryl follows suit, leaving Jordan and Brian on opposite ends of the lounge.

Brian takes her glass from her hand. "Be very careful, this abyss will fuck you up more than any drug that exists!"

She snatches her glass back. "You guys got me hooked." Brian wants to react but Jordan walks towards his room. "I need a shower." She disappears down the hallway then she returns with a question. "Are serial killers certifiable. Crazy?

"They are not crazy. They wash their cars, work at the store. They are doctors, bakers and bankers."

"Husbands, fathers and sons." She walks off to the shower.

-THIRTY-NINE-

†

Jordan enters the lounge, drying her hair with a fluffy towel. Brian turns towards the coffee maker. "I'm glad to see that you found my gown."

"Pretty soft and feminine for a man," Jordan quips, "but I like it. Fluffy and white. Do you have a set in pastels?" Brian grins. "Whatever is eating you must be suffering terribly. Coffee?"

"Nothing that boring. I would prefer something made from grapes please." Jordan sits down, draws her legs up, and reads verses from the Mariner.

> *"Ah! Well a day! What evil looks*
> *Had I from old and young!*
> *Instead of the cross, the albatross*
> *About my neck was hung."*

Brian hands her the wine. "I need a shower as well." He collects Jordan's towel and disappears down the hallway. She reads a bit before she scans his vinyl collection. Amongst the many Journey, Queen and Pink Floyd LPs, she discovers a Nat King Cole record, which she places on the turntable.

There's that signature sound of the stylus sliding into the record's groove before the irresistible smooth voice of the King fills the house. Wine glass in hand, Jordan sways to the rhythm.

> *"Unforgettable, that's what you are.*
> *Unforgettable, though near or far.*
> *Like a song of love that clings to me*
> *How the thought of you, does things to me*

Never before, has someone been more.."

Brian returns, dressed in a white T-shirt and shorts. Jordan retreats to the couch watching him as he retrieves his wine from the bar. She does a package check.

Nice legs.

"I am sorry about my emotional effusion," she starts, pulling her knees up to her chest to allow Brian access to the couch.

"You've got all the tact of a bowling ball."

Jordan sticks her tongue out at him. "Do you ever feel like you have an Albatross slumped around your neck?"

Brian scoffs. "Inspecting corpses, consoling families, diving into the cesspools of killer's fantasies, while the rest of the world is out shopping for shoes?"

"That is a profound statement. I've never given it that much thought."

"You are fortunate enough to write about the beautiful side of life. Romance, fame, fortune and fantasies. And Love. That which everyone desires and very few ever experience." Brian says, his gaze following the lines of her neck.

"How do you know what I write about? Have you read any of my novels?" Brian smiles.

"You have! I don't believe it."

"I have. And I like it."

"I have always figured you for a romantic. But don't you want fame and fortune?" She asks, pushing her cool feet underneath his warm hamstrings.

"Hey, a little fortune can't hurt. Fame, I can do without. But now I get to ask you a question. Have you ever experienced the romance that you write about?"

Jordan hesitates before she responds. "I thought I had. At first with Carl- But he faked it, I guess. But when I miscarried, he withdrew. I think he blames me."

Brian touches her foot. "I'm sorry."

"I believe in romance. You know, that initial spark? Well, I need that. I need and expect intimacy and a lot of sizzle." They laugh and hold up their glasses.

"So? Have you? Tasted intimate romance?" Jordan asks.

"I thought I might learn to love like your novels says."

There is a fragile pause. Jordan jumps up. "Dance with me." Brian takes her in his arms and they sway from side to side as Nat King starts a new song.

"When I fall in love, it will be forever
Or I'll never fall in love-"

"Most people never get to lavish in someone's soul. We choose security over intimacy, because we are anxious about being vulnerable again after a failed relationship. And then, we keep banging at each other, in more ways than one."

"Has a man ever made love to you?"

Jordan rolls her eyes. "Women get fucked mostly!" They burst out laughing, holding onto each other. There is that 'after-a-good-chuckle' moment's interlude, then Brian leans in and kisses her. Softly. Her lips resist and then give way. *God, this is nice.*

"In a restless world like this is
Love is ended before it's begun
And too many moonlight kisses
Seem to cool in the warmth of the sun"

It takes a moment for Jordan to speak again. "You are a good kisser." He kisses her again. A little more forceful. His hard chest pushing against hers.

"Enough now." She says, playfully pulling back.

Jesus, if he kisses me like that again, I'm going to fuck him!

-FORTY-

†

The charge office is quiet at 11 pm, with only the desk sergeant penning entries into the Occurrence Register when David passes by, on his way down the passage towards his office. "Hi, Sergeant. Quiet evening?"

The officer barely looks up. "Yip, let's hope it stays that way."

David unlocks his office, takes a police docket and descends the stairs into the basement area. He switches the hallway light off and walks up to the last door.

He wedges the stiff cardboard file in between the door and the top of the frame and slides it down to unlock the door's latch. He stops for a moment to listen. Positive that he is in the clear, he dons a set of gloves, enters the office, produces a flashlight and a lock pick set. He closes the door with his foot.

As the door shuts behind him, he catches a glimpse of the plaque on the door, in the light. It reads:

SAP 13 EVIDENCE STORE.

-FORTY-ONE-

†

Monet must have painted this sunrise. The vibrant orb, haloed by the dense fog, contributes to the mystical atmosphere. Hazy orange and yellow hues contrast brilliantly with the dark vessels at sea, where little if any, detail is pleasantly visible to the couple taking a romantic stroll along the shore. The mist blanketing the sand in a cold chromatic cloud may not be "beach weather," but for an expectant pair in love, it's a perfect morning.

The man propels a tennis ball as far as he can and their Border Collie, Rocky, bounds ahead. With each throw of the ball, Rocky chases gleefully, disappearing momentarily in the ethereal haze, leaving a trail of dust behind. It's his weekly exercise regime.

They manage to walk a meter or six before the Collie returns and drops the soggy ball at his master's feet. His eager tail wagging in anticipation of every motion his master makes. Amid laughter and the rhythmic sound of crashing waves, the man hurls the ball once more. But this time, Rocky's joyful barks cease, and the couple exchange puzzled glances.

"Rocky! Rocky! Come here, boy! Bring the ball!"

Anxiety creeps in as the calls for Rocky echo through the misty void. Then a distant bark reaches their ears, drawing them deeper into the mysterious daze. Guided by Rocky's echoing calls, they stumble upon a chilling discovery; a lifeless form lying on the damp sand.

The morning serenity is shattered, and replaced by a sense of dread. As they approach, the mist part to unveil the tragic scene. The body of

a naked female propped up against a bantam wall. Rocky stands beside her, his canine concern unwavering even in the face of the unknown.

Shocked and horrified, the couple exchange a silent acknowledgment that their peaceful morning had transformed into an unexpected and haunting mystery. The woman flips open her phone and starts starts dialing. The man barks an impatient command, "Rocky, come here!" and stops his wife from moving closer. "She's gone," he states the obvious, "nobody can save her."

-FORTY-TWO-

†

The diffused morning rays filter through the curtains, casting a warm serene glow on the room. Jordan stirs, her eyes opening to the realization that she was nestled in the comfort of Brian's embrace. The subtle scent of his shampoo lingers in the air, wrapping her in a cocoon of warmth. She shifts slightly, feeling the gentle rise and fall of his chest beneath her.

The sentiment that she was still clothed in his robe brings a flush to her cheeks. How did their night unfold into this delicate, intimate moment? The memories of laughter, shared stories, and stolen glances floods back, and she can't help but smile.

"Good moaning," he jokes. His husky voice filled with a hint of amusement. Brian's arms tightens around her, pulling her closer in a tender embrace. The word play doesn't escape her, and she chuckles softly.

"Good moaning, indeed," she replies, her voice carrying a teasing lilt. She turns in his arms to meet his gaze, finding a twinkle of mischief in his eyes. The connection between them is palpable, the air charged with unspoken emotions.

Brian's fingers trace delicate patterns on her back, and she sighs contentedly, losing herself in the moment. She feels a flutter in her chest, a sensation that hints at the possibility of something divinely beautiful budding between them.

"Hmm- I can get used to this." She snuggles up against him. "No sex and yet I am waking up next to a gorgeous man holding me. What is this? An arranged Marriage?"

Brian laughs. "I am no philosopher but to me, it's called intimacy." She turns to face him.

He's got a look in his eyes that you pour over waffles.

"No philosopher? That is pure poetry. What is your love language? Jordan asks.

"My primary love language is touch. Affection. Yours?"

"Hmm, aren't I a lucky girl? Mine too, and spending time together." She kisses his cheek.

"Coffee?" Brian asks just as his phone starts ringing. They walk to the kitchen while he is engaging on his cell. "Harper- Okay? Beach? Oh. I know where- Thanks."

Brian grunts when he hangs up. "They found a body on the beach not far from here. If it is our killer's work, I'll call you." Yawning, Jordan starts the coffee maker. He runs to get dressed.

WHEN BRIAN RETURNS, he finds her scribbling down notes. "New research?"

She blocks him from reading. "I just had an idea for a romantic novel."

"Is it about me?" he asks, poking her in the sides.

"I guess you'll only know if you read my books."

They exchange an intimate gaze. Jordan tries to hide behind her cup but Brian pushes it aside to kiss her. He locks the front door as he leaves. Jordan fans her face with the Mariners Rhyme, humming a Cole song until the coffee is ready. She pours a cup and skips towards the shower.

-FORTY-THREE-

†

The scolding stream stings Jordan's back like superficial needle pricks. Then she swings the faucet from hot to cold to send an energizing sensation through her body and she gives a loud, invigorating sigh. The ice water burns her skin just as much.

Thud!

A loud bang emanates from the lounge. Heart pounding, she shuts off the water with a quick twist of the knob, the drops from her wet body hitting the tiles in a muted rhythm. The house falls silent, the echoes of the sudden bang still reverberating in her ears.

"Fuck!"

She lunges for a towel, wraps herself whilst locking the bathroom door. She jumps on top of the closed toilet, the cool porcelain beneath her, tension coiling in her muscles.

Jordan strains her senses, every nerve attuned to the surrounding space. The only sound is the muffled drip of water from her damp hair onto the towel. She holds her breath, listening intently for any hint of approaching footsteps or clandestine movements from the other side of the locked door. The air in the humid bathroom hangs heavy with anticipation and dread, as she braces herself for the unknown threat that lingers just beyond the confines of the secure sanctuary she has hastily created.

She remains motionless for a while, before she puts an ear to the door.

Quite as a mouse. Because the mouse was killed in the fucking trap!

Jordan's breath is caught in her throat as she takes a few more minute to settle her nerves. With trembling hands, she opens the door just enough to peek down the hall.

That's how they get you. Impatience.

A sinister silence enveloped the house, amplifying the sound of her thumping heartbeat. She takes a deep breath, assessing the distance to Brian's room.

I can make it. What if he's in the room?

Gathering her courage, Jordan sprints into the bedroom, slams it shut and start scouring for makeshift weapons. She finds a lighter in a table drawer and seizes a can of Brian's deodorant.

My mobile is still on the couch!

Panic fuels her movements. She dressed hastily, ears strained for any hint of impending danger.

Nothing.

The eerie quiet persists. Inhaling deeply, she opens the door, ignites the flame in front of the can, and inches towards the couch. The domestic flamethrower, a technique drilled into her during self-defense classes, adds a semblance of control to her anxious state. Reaching the lounge with palms sweating and heart palpitating, Jordan peeks around the corner.

Nobody.

The room is still, save for a gentle breeze from the ajar porch door. The portrait of Brian and his father lies on the floor, the glass shattered like her sense of security. A nervous sigh escaped her lips, and a nervous giggle follows at the realization of her rather dramatic performance.

She marvels at the absurdity of employing the flamethrower technique just to retrieve her phone. It's a curious blend of anxiety and humor that leaves her feeling simultaneously empowered and ridiculous. Closing the porch door, Jordan surveys the scene. Still, the shattered portrait is an ominous reminder that danger could've breached their sanctuary. Yet, in this surreal instant, she found strength and the unexpected resourcefulness that fear had unlocked within her.

Just as she musters the courage to tackle the disaster zone, her phone rings! A scream escapes her lips that could wake the dead or at least give them a good reason to stay that way. She tries to steady herself but breaks out in a fit of hysterical laughter.

I sound like a spotted hyena.

It's Brian. She answers the call, her voice wavering between panic and amusement. "I swear my life is a sitcom."

"What?"

"I'll tell you later."

"Drive down to the pier. It's definitely our guy."

-FORTY-FOUR-

†

Cheryl pulls her Nissan Sentra into a cordoned-off parking spot behind Jordan's rented BMW. As she steps out of her car, the salty breeze carries the distant laughter of beach-goers and the rhythmic crash of waves even closer.

Jordan, with her casual charm and sunglasses perched on her head, emerges from her vehicle. They greet and cross the warm sand, passing a growing number of spectators.

The mist has fled the scene. Seagulls wheel overhead, their cries echoing the tension below.

Jordan's footsteps are muffled by the soft sand. The vibrant colors of beach umbrellas and towels just beyond the crime scene tape are complimented by the azure sky, creating a picturesque scene that contrast the darker undercurrents that often accompany a murder-suicide.

Cheryl adjusts a large manilla envelope under her arm, to free her hands and retrieve her police ID card. She displays it to the uniformed officers guarding the chevron tape. They lift the strip for the pair to proceed.

The women approach just as the Crime Scene Investigation team solemnly lifts the lifeless body to transfer it to the waiting mortuary body bag. Jordan notices that the police tape securing the perimeter shares the same yellow hue as the plastic bag protruding from the victim's mouth.

A knot tightens in Jordan's stomach as she exchanges a glance in Brian's direction. Just before they zip her up, forensics removes the evidence from her oral cavity.

"It's a shopping bag, possibly containing a substance. We'll need to run some tests to determine its composition." Cheryl says.

Brian and David wrap up a video interview with a colored woman whose excessively voluptuous figure is squashed into a pink mini-skirt and yellow boob-tube. "Now, doesn't that remind you of a cupcake spilling over the sides?" Cheryl quips. Jordan bursts out in an uncontrollable bout of laughter. "And them scuffed red platforms adds the cherry on top," she remarks.

Brian signals them closer as the prostitute slogs across the beach, kicking up a blaze of sand like a trail bike. Bemused, they watch her disappear across the dune before Brian speaks. "The victim is identified as a twenty-year-old, colored prostitute, Katriena Claassen. The killer shoved a plastic shopping bag down her throat. I can only assume it was to keep her from screaming. As per his signature, he violently sodomized and strangled her and dragged her body here."

"No cuts?" Jordan asks.

"Well, typical in an anger-retaliation crime, he acts according to the anger or disapproval he feels. He was not as upset with this girl as he was with Georginia. I believe he strangled this girl just to reach sexual satisfaction."

"Why drag her all the way here?" Jordan asks.

"Privacy I guess." Brian responds. "Necrophilia."

"Maybe he wanted us to read the graffiti?" Jordan says, pointing to the wall. "Thou shalt not steal. Maybe he wrote it?"

"I brought you a gift." Cheryl says, handing the manilla envelope over to David. He draws enlarged monochrome photographs from the envelope. He smirks before handing a photo to Jordan.

It's an image of the spectators at Prince Albert Park, and in the center of the monochrome picture is Stewart Wilken, looking straight into the lens.

"The Mariner hath his will." Jordan scoffs.

-FORTY-FIVE-

†

J ordan sits alone at her favorite corner table in the Elephant Walk, a quaint restaurant tucked away from the hustle and bustle of the urban chaos. The aroma of freshly brewed coffee mingles with the subtle notes of exotic spices, creating a comforting atmosphere that envelops her senses. A worn leather notebook lies spread-eagle, its pages filled with the scribbles of an unquiet mind.

Jordan enjoys the rhythmic clatter of keys as she types away on her laptop, each keystroke echoing the pulse of creative thinking. *The Elephant Walk* has become Jordan's haven, a refuge where the outside world fades away, leaving only the tranquil view of the city skyline.

This is my elixir for creativity.

The large windows frame a panorama of towering buildings, their steel and glass facades reflecting the changing hues of the setting sun. When daylight wanes, the city transforms into a canvas of muted tones, a perfect setting for the thriller that's unfolding in Jordan's imagination.

Since the last time, the gardeners have eradicated a Congo's worth of invasive vegetation and are now sculpting an undulating landscape of indigenous flowers and trees. Although there's a pair of burly electricians applying the finishing touches to the bar before the grand opening, she is not distracted. Neither by the lewd aromas of fine French cuisine nor the smell of roasted nuts and sugar, emanating from the chef's station.

The baked goods are a little more tricky to ignore. She capitulates. *It reminds me of Paris.*

You simply haven't lived until you have stood inside *The Boulangerie* in Paris, early morning, to take in the rich smell of bread and pastries coming out of the oven. *Arguably one of the finest smells in the world.*

Dressed in a tailored black suit, she is fully focused on creating a first draft for her novel as she traces out the road map in her notebook. Even the city below waits with baited breath for the mystery that Jordan is weaving into the fabric of its streets.

Her protagonist is a kind and intelligent profiler. She dots down bullet points relevant to the story of his backstory.

Brian places a soft kiss on the back of her head.

"So the PA gets to kiss the boss now?"

"Let me show you." Brian places a hand against Jordan's temple, draws her in and kisses her.

"I should have ordered you for lunch."

Brian takes a seat opposite her, placing his briefcase on the table. "How is your writing progressing?"

"It takes time. Tell me, was my visit reported in the news?"

Brian shakes his head. "Not that I'm aware off."

"If I tell you something do you promise not to laugh?"

"With you, I can never be sure."

"Be serious. Okay, ever since I got off the plane- I feel like I am being stalked. The incident in your place- I saw him at the pier- Do you believe me?"

"I'm taking it very serious. Can you describe the man?"

"Tall, dark complexion. Wears sunglasses and hides behind a hat. But if I see him up close, I'll know."

The waiter brings coffee. "Anyway. Let me tell you about my story. The antagonist is a serial killer. He needs to be as horrifying as hell. The leading lady is a paediatrician. Hard-working, she runs a clinic for orphans. At night, she works with the cops to save the city kids from monsters and dreadful situations. Her characters lurk in the dark as the city itself has become a character, its savage alleys and sleazy corners concealing deadly sins, begging for forgiveness."

"Brilliant," Brian responds.

"Do you have anything in your files that can cure writers block?" she says, smiling sheepishly.

Brian slides Jordan a file. The first few photos are detailed images of the corpses and potential evidence. As she flips through, she finds the image of Stewart in the crowd. She studies his eyes and his clothing.

He is square and rather stocky. Must be a strong man.

Then her eyes catch something that makes her gasp.

"What?" Brian reacts.

Jordan places the picture on the table and points to the dark figure slightly obscured by Stewart. It's a blurred image of a man in a black suit, holding a rose.

"That's him!"

-FORTY-SIX-

†

Sharon MacKenzie's cheap heels click on the pavement as she makes her way up the hill towards her house. Dressed in corporate attire, she carries a plastic bag of groceries in each hand. She stops to catch her breath before opening her gate.

"Sharon? Sharon Mackenzie?"

"Yes?" She turns around to find David and Cheryl approaching her. Cheryl presents her badge.

"What did he do now?"

"Who?"

"Stewart."

"Why do you presume that we are looking for Stewart?" David asks.

Sharon rolls her eyes and scoffs. She unlatches the gate and the trio accompany her to the door. David helps Sharon with the bags. He keeps the conversation going. "When last did you see him?"

"Not since last week-."

"Last week? Not on Wednesday? "

"Monday. I chased him away because he smoked. You don't know how he gets- Then he is the devil himself." Sharon's lip quivers. She points them towards chairs in the unkept garden. Jordan remains standing.

"Where does he stay?" David continues.

"Now? On the boat. They leave today. He will be fishing for a week."

David shoots Cheryl a look, jumps up and rushes towards their vehicle. She is taken by surprise but catches up.

"Phone Brian. He may be closer. Tell him to stop the boat!" David shouts.

When they reach the vehicle, they find the teenage girl leaning against it. David stops in front of her. "Why are you not in school."

The girl finds his comment amusing. With an unclean hand, she wipes a clump of hair from her face.

Cheryl grabs David's key and jumps in behind the wheel. She starts dialing. He walks around the car, opens the back door, grabs a bag of food, and hands it over. "Eat something," he says as he gets in.

Cheryl starts the engine. The girl checks the bag. She returns his smile.

"What's your name?" Brian asks the girl.

"Call me Nimo." She says biting into a piece of bread.

"Nimo, I'll see you later." David waves as they drive off.

Cheryl gives him a peck on the cheek. You did a beautiful thing. Do you know what the name Nimo means?

"Fish?".

"It means nobody or nothing."

"Clever girl. But we've got a boat to catch."

Then Cheryl hits the gas, hard.

-FORTY-SEVEN-

†

All 148 horses, work in unison, to pull the Mercedes C230 through the traffic on Green Street. Heart pounding, Jordan feels the adrenaline surging through her veins as Brian darts from lane to lane, squeezing the Benz into claustrophobic spaces.

It's like he's playing fucking Tetris.

Jordan had always been a bit of a thrill-seeker, but this is zenith! Despite their velocity, Brian is as calm as a Buddhist on beta-blockers, navigating traffic like an android.

A mini-bus taxi, zips across the intersection without any indication. Brian predicted its action. An instinct one quickly develops when negotiating with idiots during city driving. He hits the brakes hard enough to prevent a lock-up. Working the gears, he decelerates, then swerves into an open lane, just in time to avoid hitting the overloaded taxi.

Fuck!

Jordan is parched. Her calves are numb, her biceps are on fire from hanging on and her lower back is drenched in sweat. The car reeks of burnt rubber and battered break-pads.

Brian merges into the emergency lane, collecting several middle finger "blessings" and "positive criticism" from irate commuters. As soon as he finds an open space, he hits the gas,60, 70, then 90 kmph. Ordinarily, it's an average speed. In hostile traffic, it's loco.

The light ahead turns amber. He floors the Merc through the intersection as other drivers break hard. Brian eases off. He makes a hard right at the last second, into a side street, floors it to the next crossing and drifts into a hard left.

Jordan adjusts her position to find relief. The gravitational forces at work are playing havoc on her muscles. They tear down the narrow avenue, dodging large dustbins, at crazy speeds. They blow through several more intersections, forcing buses and trucks to swerve or stop. Again Brian brakes and pulls hard on the wheel, then uses the gas to stabilize their drift. They tear past stationary cars until the road opens up towards the harbor.

When they finally pull up to the docks, Jordan feels her legs shaking. She laughs.

The Campanile never looked more beautiful!

She giggles, sucking in oxygen, trying to calm herself.

This is what I signed up for. To feel alive again! She reminds herself.

Jordan and Brian swing the car doors open. The moment their feet hit the concrete, the distant wail of sirens becomes a crescendo, and a fleet of police vehicles skids to a stop behind them. Red and blue lights paint the surroundings in a pulsating dance of urgency.

Uniformed officers spill out of the vehicles like a well-rehearsed ensemble, swiftly taking command of the chaotic scene. They brandish yellow caution tape, efficiently cordoning off the dock with practiced precision. The atmosphere becomes charged with palpable tension as the police establish control over the unfolding stage.

Amid the orchestrated chaos, David and Cheryl sprint onto the scene.

"Brian!" David calls out, his voice cutting through the tumult. They join the duo, creating a tight-knit unit to drive
    the unfolding narrative.

"The skip is still here!" David exclaims.

"Let's go fishing," Cheryl smiles.

The clatter of the bustling dock serves as a cinematic backdrop to an impending drama. Seamen stack supplies, mechanics mend motors, and crates filled with ice are hoisted onto the boats, adding to the harbor's hive of activities.

In the center of this flurry of activity, a seemingly tranquil Stewart sits on the edge of the vessel, smoke curling lazily from his hand-rolled fag. His legs dangle casually over the side, indifferent to the hectic scene around him. Then the persistent call of David pierces through the commotion. "Stewart! Stewart!"

Stewart looks up to see the bedlam. He rises with measured calmness, retrieving a tray laden with knives. Two gleaming fillet knives find a place by his sides. He turns to take a long look at the inviting waters, but to Jordan's horror, Stewart swings around and starts to approach Cheryl and David with purpose.

The clinks and clatters of the dock continue, unaware of the tension building.

"Stop! Put it down, Stewart. I need to talk to you." David commands, his voice cutting through the ambient noise.

A boat's engine roars to life, and a plume of diesel smoke billows across the harbor, momentarily obscuring Jordan's view of Stewart. The acrid smog dances in the air, adding an eerie dimension to the unfolding scene. Stewart, unfazed, shifts his advance towards Cheryl.

"Stewart, drop the knife," warns David, a note of urgency in his voice. Uniformed officers, vigilant and poised, cock and aim their shotguns at the stocky suspect.

Stewart persists in his approach, undeterred. Cheryl, sensing the gravity of the situation, places her hand on her sidearm and calls out to him. "Don't be stupid. Halt!"

Stewart stops, his gaze shifting between the boats and the open sea, as if searching for a possible escape route. With cautious determination, he inches forward.

David, sensing the escalating tension, draws his weapon. "I want to talk to you about Henry."

The boat's engine sighs into silence, and the hectic harbor succumbs to an eerie hush. The dockworkers, previously an ensemble of motion and clattering tools, now stand frozen in an otherworldly stillness, as if time itself is holding its breath. The able seamen, caught in mid-action, resemble a tableau of cast and crew on pause, awaiting the elusive command from an unseen director to break the spell.

The seagulls, tireless spectators of the maritime theater, have not conceded the stage to silence. Their squawks echo through the air, a cacophony reminiscent of fervent supporters at a football match. With each call, they seem to rally, hanging in the vast expanse of the sky like loyal fans, awaiting the kickoff of a match in the harbor below. They are keenly aware that the impending spectacle will be nothing short of extraordinary.

Stewart, his face a canvas of conflicting emotions, hesitates as the last flimsy veil of machine smoke dissipates. Then, as clarity cuts through the haze, his eyes lock onto Jordan. Recognition dawns like a slow sunrise, casting light on the shadows of doubt.

Brian, ever the observer, follows Stewart's line of sight. His expression morphs from curiosity to disbelief in an instant. "Oh God"

The moment stretches, suspended in the vacuum of realization. Stewart, torn between worlds, pivots on the axis of a choice. Without a word, he turns his back on David, the clatter of knives hitting the ground a punctuation mark in the profound silence. His hands, once steady, now rise to cradle his head as if trying to contain the storm within.

"On your knees!" David's authoritative voice slices through the stillness. He moves with purpose, his steps deliberate as he closes the distance. Cuffs jangle, and the pat-down begins- the procedural dance of law enfolding a man in the embrace of justice. It's a cue for the crews to continue with their day.

"I am going to read you your rights," Cheryl informs Stewart. David picks up on the trace of enjoyment in her voice. Stewart ignores her completely. His voice pierces through, a desperate plea wrapped in confusion.

"Emma? Are you my sister, Emma?" His eyes, haunted and searching, fixate on Jordan. "I always dream about you."

-FORTY-EIGHT-

†

LOUIS LE GRANGE SQUARE. PORT ELIZABETH. 1997.
The trip to the charge office is a quick one. Louis Le Grange Square has a cold, austere look. The architecture is typical of many old government buildings; ten stories of steel, pale brick, and mortar. What makes it unique is a reserved elevator that only stops at level five- the classified floor of the security branch. Here, they play host to VIP prisoners in simple steel cages.

The guests used to be enemies of the state, but now it's reserved for the most wanted. Jordan watches from Brian's vehicle as Stewart emerges from the back of the yellow police van. He presents the image of an anxious child.

"And are you going to lock me up with other people?" He asks David.

David is soft-spoken. "We are going to talk first. So I need you to be truthful, okay Stewart?"

Two uniformed officers escort Stewart into the precinct. The quartet meet up. Cheryl lights a cigarette. David paces around. "I believe this is my guy."

"He most certainly matches the profile."

"What's our strategy?" Brian probes, his eyes narrowing. David draws hard and long on the cigarette; the smoke hangs in the air, a veil of contemplation.

He exhales slowly, the tendrils curling upward like wisps of secrecy. "Give me five minutes, then bring him to my office," David says, his words carrying the weight of a carefully devised plan.

-FORTY-NINE-

†

David feverishly shifts and stacks case files against his office's wall, the room filled with the rustle of paper. He then rearranges the furniture, ensuring Stewart is facing the wall adorned with David's achievements, photos, and diplomas in police profiling.

"Did you notify them?" David checks, his eyes scanning the room for any details he might have missed.

Cheryl aims a Betamax camera toward the empty chair, adjusting the lens with precision. "Yes. They are bringing him up. "Ready?"

David runs a final check. "Ready. Please send him in." Cheryl starts the recording, steps out and returns, escorting a cuffed Stewart. David points Stewart to the chair. "Have a seat, Stewart. Can we get you something to drink.

Stewart sits down, the cold metal of the cuffs clinking as he moves. "Coke." David stands in front of the wall to ensure Stewart sees the diplomas. "I need some coffee, then we can talk."

They leave Stewart alone in the office. Stewart sits motionless, staring at his shoes. It takes a while before he looks up. His gaze travels from the video camera across to the wall. As he reads, he mouths the words of the credentials on every certificate.

Then his eyes move to the portrait of a happy little girl smiling at him. His eyes well up, emotions bubbling to the surface like a storm breaking through a calm sea.

The room remains still; the ticking of a clock is the only audible sound. Stewart's past and present collide within the confines of David's office, setting the stage for a conversation that will unravel the threads of a captivating narrative.

-FIFTY-

†

Jordan is completely immersed in structuring her notes, her focus unwavering, oblivious to all the activity taking place behind her in the monitor room. The hum of technology surrounds her, but she's lost in her own world.

Cheryl, on the other hand, is busy connecting audio-video cables to a monochrome video monitor. She hits the *On* switch, and the screen takes a second or more to warm up before revealing Stewart's image. His face is cast in the cold glow of the monitor.

As David enters the room Brian questions him, "Why are you here? You should be in there."

"I have a hunch," David declares, his eyes fixed on the screen, "I think I can get him to open up. I am giving him some rope."

Jordan looks up, her brows furrowed. "What's he looking at?" They turn their attention to the monitor, where Stewart is still staring at the wall, seemingly lost in thought. Jordan frowns.

"At my diplomas," David replies, a hint of realization dawning on him.

"I think it is something else. He is emotional," Jordan observes, her analytical mind kicking into gear. "Emotions, memories, and a connection to the past might be the key to unlocking-" A smile spreads across David's face. "That's it!"

-FIFTY-ONE-

†

Stewart hears the distinct laughter of a little girl. It's undoubtedly the joyful noise of a girl enjoying the time spent with her father, building sandcastles on the beach. It's the laughter that emanates from within the beautiful girl's soul, and it erupts.

Stewart is instantly jerked back to the present when David enters the room. He hands Stewart a soda. "You see, this is how it works. I ask some questions, and then you test me with some lies." Stewart glances up at David. His eyes move back to the portrait. "It always happens. Always. Everybody tries to cover their sins by lying."

Inside the monitor room, Jordan moves her chair closer to the monitor, still trying to gauge what Stewart finds so mesmerizing. Stewart lowers his head again, staring at the floor. The monitor's low-quality speaker adds a lot of treble to David's voice. Cheryl adjusts the volume.

"But- I already have so many answers that you are going to look like a fucking moron," David continues. Stewart slowly raises his head. He looks David dead in the eye, and in the softest tone, he says, "I am sick."

The weight of his words sinks into the room like an anchor plunging into the depths of the sea.

The distinct sound of the harbor bell tolling in the distance resonates, a somber echo accompanying the revelation. *The New Dawn's* horn announces that it's departing the safety of the port as it heads out toward uncharted waters.

-FIFTY-TWO-

†

"There passed a weary time. Each throat
Was parched, and glazed each eye.
A weary time! a weary time!
How glazed each weary eye,"
- The Rime of the Ancient Mariner

David removes his firearm and locks it in the safe. "Don't you want a lawyer present?" David checks with Stewart before he places his chair opposite the mariner. They sit almost knee-to-knee.

"No."

David exhales sharply. "This isn't a game, Stewart. You're facing serious charges-"

"Do you want to see them?"

David leans back, studying Stewart. Stewart's gaze remains fixed on the tabletop. His jaw tightens.

"Do you want to see them?" He mutters, slowly rising from his seat. Standing over David he bellows, "I'm Boetie Boer! Do you want to see all of the bodies?"

The weight of his confession lingers, it hangs in the air like an end-of-days message.

I've got you.

There's a faint knock at the door. David sighs. He gets up and Stewart slumps back into his seat. Cheryl pops her head in. She grin she wears resembles a drugged-up version of the Cheshire cat. "I have Wilken's arrest warrant for non-appearance." They step into the hallway where Jordan is engaged in a cellphone call.

Cheryl grabs David around the neck and kisses his cheek. David smiles when she lets go of him. He scrolls through the warrant. "Grab his coke bottle and let the guys take a DNA swab."

They return to Stewart, leaving the door ajar. Cheryl collects the bottle and as she exits, Jordan ends the call. She looks up to see Stewart staring straight at her.

David closes the door, takes his seat and centers himself before he speaks. "You did not attend court." He places the warrant on the table in front of Stewart. Stewart ignores it like a stop sign.

"Can we talk about these boys?" David asks.

"Oh okay," Stewart thinks before he continues, "that first boy wanted food for a fuck."

"First boy?" David instantly recognizes that he was not referring to one of Veronica's sons.

"The boy from the school in Sydenham."

Bingo!

"Do you remember his name?"

"I didn't ask. And I don't remember him telling me."

"When was this?"

"Long ago, about four years and he came to me and I said no, and left but he followed me."

"Where did you go?"

Stewart senses the kink in David's armor. The desperation to hear his confession. It's not that Stewart is reluctant to share his story, quite the contrary, he has now recognized a chance to manipulate. An opportunity for trade-offs.

He leans back in his chair again.

"Give me another coke and call in the cop with the blond hair and I want to tell her everything."

-FIFTY-THREE-

†

"I don't think you should even consider it," Brian answers, trying to control his tone. David drives his point. "If he confesses then I- We wrap this case up, tonight."

"It's not about that-"

"I have been busting my balls for years on this, Brian."

"It's not about you."

David gets up into Brian's face. "Well, fuck knows, it may be time that it's about me. What about Cheryl? She needs a break too. It's about getting this monster off the streets," David grumbles.

Cheryl starts, "David-"

"What's the worst that can happen?" David interrupts her. "He confesses to Jordan what she already knows? Come on!"

Brian slams his palms against the wall. Jordan strolls into the conflict zone before Brian can answer. "What's going on?"

David shoots Brian a look. Brian faces the wall.

"Is this a discussion about me? I wondered where you lot disappeared to-"

David interrupts. "Sis, how would you feel about sitting in with the interrogation?"

"What? Can I?"

"Only as an observer." Brian turns to face Jordan. "He said he'll spill the beans if you sit in. But there is a certain amount of risk involved."

"Is he cuffed?" She asks.

"Yes." David answers.

"Then where is the danger?"

128

"I am only saying," Brian sighs. "mainly psychological stress. This could screw with your mind! Jordan, this is what *diving into the abyss* means."

"Is there a chance of saving Harry and Wuané?"

Brian avoids eye contact. "He is about to expose you to his tortured soul, to every perverse fantasy."

"Is there a chance of saving those two kids?"

"You will share the waters with every victim because it is his ego at work."

Jordan shoves her mobile under Brian's chin. "Answer me. Is there a chance of saving Harry and Wuané?"

He looks her in the eye. "Maybe. Yes. But it's not about anything but him. I don't think you should-"

"I tend agree with Brian," Cheryl adds.

"I just want to protect you from a level of perversion-"

"You didn't just say that." Jordan moves away from Brian. "I don't need another champion to save me. I took this decision- The responsibility to write this book and come hell or high water, I am going to complete it."

"It may be more hell water, than high water." Brian surrenders.

Jordan scoffs, charges into the monitor room and returns with a notepad and pencil. She snaps at Brian. "Sounds like the water temperature that I have become accustomed to."

She taps her brother on the shoulder.

"Lead me into the abyss, brother!"

-FIFTY-FOUR-

†

Stewart fails to cut an imposing figure.
He's no Hannibal Lecter.

The difference, however, is that this is not Hollywood. It's not a flick. This is a man who kills with impunity. Because of this reality, Jordan's body language betrays her trepidation the moment they make eye contact. She looks away to gather herself.

The air in the room seems to hold its breath, suspended, as if unwilling to exhale. Brian enters and moves his chair into the corner. David starts speaking, then resists. He clears his throat instead and takes a seat next to the camera. Stewart's gaze remains fixed on Jordan, an unsettling intensity emanating from his cold, calculating eyes. His thin lips curl into a sinister smile that fails to put anyone at ease. He lounges back in his chair, casual yet commanding, a stark contrast to the gravity of the situation.

Jordan opts to move her chair near the door, strategically positioning herself for both observation and escape if needed.

Stewart, seemingly attuned to the palpable tension, breaks the uneasy silence without turning around. His voice, a low, chilling whisper, cuts through the stillness.

"And come and sit here." The interviewer's chair scrapes across the floor as he pulls it closer with a nonchalant sweep of his foot.

Jordan, however, declines to succumb to the manipulation. She squares her shoulders and meets Stewart's eyes with a determined stare, but the unease lingers beneath the surface.

The door opens, and Colonel Claassen enters, followed by a gentleman in a dark suit. "Everybody, this is Mr. Alwyn Griebenow, council for Mister Wilken." Griebenow moves to speak to Stewart. "Do you wish to speak to me first?" he whispers.

"I'm okay."

"Do you want me to represent you?"

"Yes, okay."

"Have your rights been made clear?" "Yes."

"Do you understand your rights?" "Yes!"

"I can only represent you and not defend you if you wish to carry on."

Claassen moves in front of Stewart to ensure that the camera captures the interaction. "I have requested that a lawyer be present. Mr. Wilken, I have to remind you that your rights still apply. Do you understand that and do you wish to continue?"

"Yes."

Griebenow sighs. "May I begin by stating that my client is making the statement out of his own free will and that he desires to do so. He understands that he can end the interview at any time as well, should he wish to do so."

Stewart doesn't react. Cheryl gets the camera rolling.

"Where's Em- the blonde detective? I can't see you. I want to tell you what happened to them." Stewart calls.

Jordan hesitates, caught between defiance and caution. Her eyes flicker towards Brian, seeking guidance. His subtle gesture urges her to remain where she is- a silent promise of protection. Jordan changes to the chair in front of Stewart, opens her notebook and starts tapping in an anxious rhythm with her pen.

Cheryl rolls the camera and David kicks off the interview.

"You wanted to talk to me about a boy?"

Stewart stares directly into the camera lens. "Yes."

"A fifteen-year-old boy, In 1990? Do you know his name?" "No."

"Monte. Monte Fiko?"

"Monte. Yes!" Stewart exclaims, his voice echoing with a theatrical enthusiasm that belongs to a contestant on a high-stakes game show. The words burst forth from him, charged with a strange mix of excitement and menace, as if he's just revealed a hidden ace in a twisted deck of cards.

"Why?" The word escapes Jordan's lips.

Stewart leans forward. His eyes gleam with a predatory glint, and a sinister smile plays on his lips. The air in the room shifts, thickening with an unsettling energy.

"I can see their skeletons. And then I want to take the skin off." There is a beat before Stewart speaks again, slowly and purposefully.

"And he asked me for food, and so he said that we must go to that school."

"Which school are you referring to?" Jordan asks.

"I don't know that name."

"Cillié High school?"

"Cillié. And we went to smoke marijuana there and then he took his pants off and I told him how to suck my cock."

Stewart touches himself as he seeks a reaction from Jordan. She ignores his statement and pretends to jot down a note in her book.

Jesus!

Jordan continues. "Did you tell him or show him?

"And he sucked me and I came into his mouth and I took off his pants."

"And then?"

"And I fuck him and I put my cock in him and I fuck him and then he cried and said he was going to tell the police that I fuck him."

"Yes?"

"And then I gave him Fifty Rands and he screamed and I became scared." Jordan keeps writing.

He became scared? The fucking irony!

"And they already told the police I fucked other two boys."

"What happened next?"

"And I felt sorry for him because he did not have a good life at his house, and they always kicked him and beat him like a dog and he was on the streets most of the time."

"Yes?"

"So I wanted to help him." "How did you help him?" "I sent him back to God."

"Does that mean you killed him?"

"He is with Jesus now."

"Can you demonstrate how you did it?"

"Gladly." Stewart's voice is a low, guttural growl that sends shivers down Jordan's spine. A shadow draws across his face, accentuating the sinister contours of his features.

Stewart rises, his groin on Jordan's level, and an involuntary shudder runs through her. The putrid odor permeating the man's aura makes her stomach churn- a sickening blend of malice and decay.

She can feel the weight of Brian's gaze on her, her pulse racing. Her mind is a chaotic whirlwind of fear and revulsion, but she forces herself to maintain eye contact with the psychopath.

"He was lying on his back, and I took his belt and put it around his neck."

Brian and David exchange wary glances, silently communicating their readiness to intervene at the slightest provocation.

David interrupts. "Did you sodomize the boy after you strangled him?" Stewart's gaze intensifies, searching Jordan's face for a reaction. "I fuck him again, yes."

She fights to maintain a facade of composure, concealing the terror bubbling beneath the surface. He smirks, a chilling expression that sends a chill down Jordan's spine.

"Did you put the newspaper in his anus?" David asks.

The room has become a pressure cooker. a battleground of wills, and Jordan realizes that she's dancing on the precipice of something far more sinister than she could have ever imagined. Stewart sits down without breaking eye contact with Jordan.

Poker face!

"If they enjoyed fucking- I put the paper in there, to keep the flies out."

David pushes through. "So you went back to the boys."

Stewart loses interest in the conversation. He is now fixated on Jordan. "And do you want to ask me something more? What is your name, detective?"

Her stomach gives out a rumble.

"Meaning?"

Her eyes flicker and then Jordan slowly rises to tower over Stewart. She speaks softly, as if addressing a little boy.

"My name is Jordan, not Emma. I am not your sister. I am not a detective, I am a writer. Do you understand, son?"

Her approach completely takes the wind out of Stewart's sails.

"Yes, Ma'am."

"I want to know who you are. Only if we respect each other."

"My name is Boetie."

"Good to meet you." She grabs onto her chair, slips down, organizes her thoughts, then opens with a generic question.

"Tell me about yourself. Where did you grow up?"

"In a small house in Boksburg, and Oom Doep isn't really my uncle; he just collected children to get government money, and he didn't work, and Emma and I used to play outside in the dirt."

Jordan leans forward, her pen poised over the notepad. "Where is Emma?"

"Our mother came to fetch her and I didn't want to go and I don't know where she is."

"What about your mother?"

"She's a whore. She shows up and takes Emma away. Oom Doep didn't like it, but he never said much and Emma and I, we just stuck together, you know?"

Jordan nods, absorbing the raw emotion in Stewart's voice. "And your father?"

His eyes narrow, a flicker of resentment crossing his face. "I don't remember much about that. All I know is what Oom Doep told me. He said my father was a no-good drunk who couldn't handle the responsibility of three kids. And so he left us there, and Oom Doep found us before anything bad could happen."

"Did your father ever come back?"

A bitter chuckle escapes Stewart. "Good riddance, I say."

He looks away and then back at Jordan, a haunted conviction clouds his features. ""There are fallen ones with us," Stewart begins, his eyes scanning her face, "they are the watchers and they stay here to torture us."

-FIFTY-FIVE-

†

B OKSBURG. 1968.
The Highveld deluge ended as abruptly as it arrived, permeating the air with the pleasant aroma of wet earth. The echo of distant thunder signals its departure.

Doep's house is devoid of pulse. Instead of breath, there is mold. The transistor radio in the lounge broadcasts to an audience of one. The start of the evening news is evidence that it's just gone past 7 pm.

"Boeing confirmed today that South African Airways Flight 228, which crashed in Windhoek, was due to pilot error."

As Doep extends an arm to turn the volume up, there is a loud knock on the front door. "Fuck!" he exclaims. He detests a disturbance when the news is on.

"Coming!" He banishes the thought of putting on a shirt as he attempts to capture the headlines while edging toward the door. The visitor bangs the door insistently.

"I'm coming!" Doep removes the door chain.

"The Boeing 707, which was only six weeks old, flew into the ground soon after take-off, killing 123 people including the pilot, Captain Eric Smith."

Doep plucks the door open and comes face to face with two burly Police officers. Their navy blue uniform blazers, adorned with bronze buttons, match their pressed trousers and trimmed mustaches. Polished black shoes, boned to repel water, rounds off a commanding ensemble.

Sergeant Du Toit lays a large hand on the door and forcefully steps into the lounge followed by Constable Roos as well as two civilians, Mister & Misses Wilken.

Doep stumbles back and before he is able to utter a word, the Sergeant marshals his group through the house. The Constable operates the light switches as they advance and scout the place.

They reach the back door. Doep collapses into a kitchen chair, and lights a cigarette between his stained fingers.

Roos returns to keep Doep company. Du Toit turns to the female. "Misses Wilken?"

Petronella Wilken leads the officer into a wet courtyard litterer with vehicle spares and oil cans. She points to a wonky dog house. Du Toit shines his flashlight into the box. They can hear a puppy grunting inside.

Suddenly, a fox terrier scampers out and runs away, tail tucked between his legs. The grunting has ceased.

There is a frayed rope tied to the outside of the dog house, leading to an animal still on the inside. The Sergeant kneels and traces the line with his hand, pulling gently until he gets to the other end. On the other end, he finds the puppy.

It is a human puppy.

The rope is knotted around the human's neck.

The petrified human looks up at Petronella. She removes her coat and entices the trembling boy to leave the security of the foul, damp box. He gradually crawls into the snug garment.

His fragile little body is riddled with lesions, scabs and he's infested by colonies of lice, flees and parasites. A bleak canvas exhibiting the horrific existence he is subjected to.

Most prominent, are the round sores concentrated around his genitalia and buttocks. Scorch marks made by cigarettes being extinguished against exposed flesh.

Mr. Wilken takes the bundle from his wife. "Let's get him home."

Somewhere inside the grimy kitchen, Doep sobs like a baby.

-FIFTY-SIX-

†

LOUIS LE GRANGE SQUARE. PORT ELIZABETH. 1997.
Brian and David find Jordan pacing the courtyard at the back
of the precinct. Her lips pressed in a tight line. She only seem to relax
when David hugs her.

"You did great in there," he says.

She laughs, then playfully punches Brian's shoulder. "See? It's not
that hard. And you thought I wouldn't be able to swim through the
abyss."

He pulls her closer to him. "I'm sorry I doubted you both-" Cheryl
interrupts their celebration. "David." She hands him a court order. "The
charges against Wilken have been dropped by his in-laws."

"Fuck!" David lets slip.

"What does that mean?" Jordan asks.

"We can't keep him any longer. He can walk."

"But he confessed, didn't he?"

"He started, but then he switched over to narrating his life's story.
And I'm not fucking the case up. I want every T crossed."

"What now?"

David turns to Cheryl. "What did his lawyer say?"

"He also stepped out. So, I don't know." Cheryl responds.

"Let's get back." David sets off at a brisk pace. "I need Stewart to
confess. I'll take over and push the interview."

"I don't think so," Jordan says, "if you take over, he'll shut down."

"Then you'll have to draw the confession out of him. And quickly."

"Stewart the man will give you nothing. You can't push. Let me do it my way."

They come to a halt outside the office. David scratches his sideburns. "I need this!"

"We need the children back safe."

"I agree with Jordan," Brian says. Cheryl nods. Jordan touches David's arm. "I am skilled in the art of conducting interviews. I do it often. Every time, before writing a novel." David rubs his chin hard.

"Fuck it!"

"If I can break through to the boy in him, he'll tell me what we need to know."

David makes a quick 360 before grabbing the door handle.

"We are so close. Let's not fuck this up."

-FIFTY-SEVEN-

†

A jovial Stewart enters like a celebrity boarding a yacht. Jordan fidgets with her pen.

Click! Click! Click!

Despite being used to interviewing celebs, Jordan can't shake the feeling of suddenly being overwhelmed.

It feels like my first time.

She studies Stewart's demeanor as he engages with his attorney and the police officers.

Napoleon complex! That's it!

But even that epiphany doesn't tip the scales, when Stewart takes his seat close to her. His overwhelming odor stings her nostrils.

That Napoleon needs loo water.

Jordan endeavors to avoids eye contact, seeking courage from her team and finding it in Brian's eyes. Stewart bends down to collect a piece of hair from the floor, wipes his nose on his grimy green sweater and hides the hair up his sleeve. Cheryl signals the start of the interrogation. "Camera rolling."

Jordan breathes in. "We ended our conversation when you were taken from Doep. Take us through-"

"No, no, no," Stewart interrupts, "I want to tell you about the other boy." Griebenow gets up. "Mr. Wilken?" Jordan shoots a look towards David and Cheryl's tense faces.

"The boy wanted me to go to that place where we played cricket against the Aussies and the Charras- The Indians."

"Is that St. Georges park?" Jordan asks.

"Yes, yes. That's the place! And so we went to smoke and suck and then he wants money. And he hits me with a stick and I slapped him down, then I squeezed his neck."

"Did you strangle him with your hands?"

"Did you find him already or must I show you?"

Cheryl nods and Jordan confirms the answer. "Yes we did. We'll let you show us all the places later." Jordan checks her notes.

"Was that back in 1991? October?"

"Yes. And did you find the one at Target Kloof?"

"We found the body of a young boy of about fourteen."

"In the ravine! Yes! I did fuck him. I paid him but it wasn't good because he did not relax," Stewart says matter-of-factly, "and I strangled him to get him to relax- And when the eyes goes *boof!* and puffs up and then I can cum easily." Stewart shifts in his seat, reliving the moment.

Every fiber of Jordan's being protests, pleading for this narrative to stop. She grinds her pencil into the notepad.

Silence. She looks up to find David grinning from ear to ear. He gives her the thumbs up.

"And the boy at the fort?"

David shrugs. Jordan is surprised to hear her own voice asking, "The Fort?"

"I'll tell you if you take me there."

-FIFTY-EIGHT-

†

During the day, Fort Frederick stands guard over the magnificent view of Algoa Bay and it's a place for romantic talks, walks and tourist selfies. Erected by British troops to prevent a possible Napoleonic landing, the fort houses a powder magazine and a blockhouse built with the rocks from the natural citadel on which it is perched.

It was defended by two 8-pounder guns and one 5.5-inch Howitzer. Till this day, no retributive shots had been fired from the impotent weapons, placed across barren walls.

The fort, however, becomes a very different place during the dark hours. When the haves are safely locked up, the have-nots roam free. It's a place of predators and prey.

Tonight, the predator, the fallen will reveal the remains of its victim-the meek.

Jordan wrings her fingers. David takes hold of her hands.

"It's almost over, tomorrow we'll speak to Petronella Wilken and Lynn Havenga. Then you can write your book."

Brian pours a refreshing cup of Joe from a metal flask and hands it to her. "This will warm your bones."

The CSI team flood the citadel with spotlights for those commandeered to attend the advent. The coroner's *wagon* arrives and a news crew pitch up to capture B-roll footage.

"Who called the news crew? Fuck no."

Special Task Force officers secure ropes on the southern incline, in case they need to abseil the descending Baakens Valley ravine. A jovial

Stewart is set free from the vehicle and his cuffs. He runs two fingers across his thick mustache, wipes his hands on his soiled sweater, adjusts his white beanie and immediately engages with Jordan.

"And I put him over the edge."

Griebenow sighs, Jordan discards the last coffee from her mug, flips her collar up and pulls her bandana over her nose. The TV cameras start recording.

Show time.

Stewart leads the entourage toward the ravine. "And I left him here," he says, pointing towards the southern wall of the fort.

"Over the drop-off?" Jordan exclaims.

Stewart laughs. "No, just on the side."

Two officers rappel down the steep embankment and anchor the rope. This allows David, Stewart and then Jordan to employ the cord like a handrail as he descends the incline. Stewart finds the location with ease. He removes a dried bush to reveal a severely decomposed body. "Here he is." He calls out.

The CSI team descends upon the decaying crime scene like vultures drawn to a morbid feast. Jordan collects mental data, carefully studying their protocols. Their movements- calculated, their focus unwavering. Their gloved hands deftly collecting biological samples, lifting latent prints, and meticulously cataloging trace evidence.

The flash of the camera illuminates the darkness, freezing the scene in a series of stark, haunting images. Jordan can already imagine how much weight each photograph, each frame capturing this moment of horror, will be dissected and analyzed in the pursuit of justice.

SWAT officers assist Jordan, David and Stewart back up. The TV crew identifies her as her bandana slips and there is a commotion to capture footage of Jordan. The journalists plead, argue and bargain with the officers because they are held at bay and can't get to Stewart on his way back to the cop cars. By the time they reach Jordan's position, Stewart is short of breath.

"I can't believe it. He's still here. Have you decided to write a book about me?"

"Is that Henry?"

Stewart shrugs. Shakes his head.

"Is this where you strangled him?" David asks.

Stewart looks at Jordan. "He wanted to run to tell the fucking pigs-Police. And I caught him and he didn't think I was that quick. And then I fuck him and I took him inside and strangled him. And we slept here and the next morning I put him there. And I put vinegar and butter on his feet."

"Why?"

"And that the police dogs can't find him." He smiles.

"Did you return to him? To have sex?"

"Yes, even when there were people here, I was here."

Jordan shudders, but not from the cold breeze cutting through her. The officers start to move Stewart toward the patrol car.

"Stewart?" Jordan calls out. He turns around. "How many have you killed?"

Stewart takes a moment before he replies. "We have sent ten to God."

-FIFTY-NINE-

†

If there is one thing the sixty year old Alice loves more than the SABC news, it's when Riaan Crywagen anchors the Afrikaans news.

Her apartment, a living testament to another era, cocoons her in nostalgia. Stagnant brown furniture, remnants of a bygone era, sits stoically, bearing witness to the passage of time. Knick-knacks perch on surfaces, each telling a story of a moment frozen in the amber of memory. Except for the Phillips TV, nothing new has entered her sacred space. Not even a man.

Alice's weary fingers trace the contours of the remote control, a well-worn extension of her hand, as she navigates through the channels. The SABC 2 news intro fades, and there he is- Riaan.

As he delivers the headlines in his resonant baritone, Alice reaches for a pack of cigarettes, a familiar companion in her solitary moments. With practiced ease, she lights one, and the ember glows in the dimly lit room. Smoke curls lazily into the air, dancing its own waltz as if in harmony with the reporter's voice.

"Police decline to comment at this stage but the suspect is a homeless man who is known to the locals as Boetie Boer."

Alice pushes the volume up. The ash at the tip of her cigarette elongates, defying gravity for a moment, as she forgets the ritual of tapping it into the ashtray.

The camera, a voyeur to the unfolding spectacle, sweeps towards the suspect, a figure in distress being escorted to a waiting patrol car. Alice's eyes widen, her pupils dilating with the intensity of her attention. She leans forward, as if proximity to the screen could reveal more than the pixel resolution allows.

With a sudden burst of realization, she lifts her middle finger, a solitary conductor orchestrating the movements of her spectacles. Pushing them up over the bridge of her nose, she mumbles, almost in disbelief, "Oh my god!" The cigarette ash crashes to the floor and she coughs up another mouth full of phlegm.

-SIXTY-

†

"God, this is draining," Jordan sighs, her voice carrying a weariness that hangs in the air like a heavy perfume. Her finger taps rhythmically on the glass, a restless dance born of impatience or perhaps a subtle manifestation of her underlying frustration. Across the table, Brian catches the rhythm, his eyes meeting hers in a shared sentiment.

A few friendly expressions exchanged with the waiter becomes a silent language, a wordless request for respite in the form of another gin cocktail. A wink of understanding passes between them, a fleeting acknowledgment of the order received.

"Let's make it a second round for me as well, please," Brian declares, a hint of a smile playing on his lips. The waitress nods in agreement.

"How you keep going, I don't know." Jordan scans the bar and its informal patrons. At the end of the bar, a woman sits, smoking and contemplating.

That cigarette looks inviting.

"I like this place, lively atmosphere. Here you can liquidate your convictions."

Jordan realizes that she's rambling and that Brian is looking at her with a tenderness she recognizes.

"I'm sorry I snapped at you. My-" The waitress delivers the spirits. Generic pause. The waitress collects the hollow glasses and with a "Thank you," she disappears.

"My lawyer called- When we were at the precinct. My divorce has gone through. And for some or other reason I became upset when I should have felt relieved?" Brian touches her hand.

"But, I don't want to discuss it. I just needed to apologize to you. Please keep me focused on completing my book."

"I am your PA, am I not?" Brian digs.

"You will make a great researcher for an author- Like me." She digs back.

"Oh, wink, wink! You may be too fierce a boss."

"It is my worst quality. I get defensive when I'm pressured."

Brian raises his glass. "Then you would have been a cage fighter, if you were in my profession." They chuckle.

"Do you think it's strange that I have empathy, even compassion, for Stewart?" Again he takes Jordan's hand in his.

I like it when he does that.

"Stewart's life unfolded like a tragic tapestry, woven with threads of atrocious interactions," Jordan continues, "and none of the adults intervened to protect him."

Brian squeezes her hand gently, a silent reassurance that transcends words. "You succeeded in reaching the boy inside of him. But he is not a boy anymore."

"I know. Yet I sense a vulnerability in him. Maybe because of Wuané. Do you think he knows where she is?"

Brian, ever pragmatic, responds with a suggestion that cuts through the uncertainty. "Why don't you ask him?" It's a challenge and an invitation rolled into one.

"We found Stewart. I believe we will find Henry and Wuané as well," Jordan asserts her conviction.

In the charged silence that follows, Brian leans in, closing the distance between them. The weight of their shared mission momentarily set aside, he kisses Jordan.

-SIXTY-ONE-

†

"As far as I can see, this is heaven
And speaking just for me, it's ours to share"

"**I** came here over for a nightcap, why are we dancing?" She asks, swaying to the seductive songs of Johnny Mathis.

"Because we can," Brian answers, drawing her closer, "and because I like being this near to you." He says softly before he kisses Jordan. He starts with a tender kiss which becomes a little firmer, keeping a subtle mouth while moving from her bottom lip to the top one.

I want to be kissed like this forever.

"Have I told you that you are a great kisser? Oh yes, I have."

"Have I told you how beautiful you are to me?" Brian places his hand against Jordan's cheek.

"Tell me," she whispers.

"You have the most beautiful, kind eyes, inviting pools of Jade. You have a most magical smile, an addictive laugh and the most kissable mouth, and god, I love your taste and the way you move."

He moves his hand to the back of her head and kisses Jordan until reason seeps out through her pores and she becomes a living pulse, conscious only of what she needs him to do to her. His mouth travels down to her neck, leaving nips along the way.

"You make me weak," she whispers.

He moves to kiss her along her collarbone and back up to her throat.

Oh god, the feel of him, his scent, his taste!

149

He unbuttons her blouse, twisting each button with his thumb and third finger, one by one. Patiently, unwrapping a gift.

When her shirt finally falls open, he admires her, running the palm of his hand along her breastbone, around her throat and up to her chin. She drapes her arms around his neck. Her kiss is unbearably fragile and tender, flicking her tongue across his lips. Brian's hands slip around her waist, spiking fresh sensations. Her lips stay on his as she opens his shirt.

Skin on skin.

Her mouth tells him everything, without saying a word.

Brian hands her her wine, then leads her to his room, where she steps out of her shoes. He lights a pair of scented candles. He draws her in with his hand on the small of her back. Jordan pushes her hands underneath his shirt and across his shoulders. The garment drops to the floor. She runs her hand across his shaven chest in a slow design.

"So what would your pet name be for me?" she asks, nuzzling her face against his hard pecks, realizing as she did so, her heightened desire for the scents and textures of his skin.

"Jade," he says without hesitation. "Jade, the captivating color in your eyes."

"Hmm- I love that. Say it."

"Jade," he whispers, "beautiful Jade."

She runs her tongue over his nipples moving up to his mouth. She feels his body responding to the excitement of her tender, tickling licks and kisses.

Brian kisses her with a firm mouth. His hands travel up the small of her back, pops the clips of her bra before gently moving the straps off her shoulders, letting the lingerie fall. She closes her eyes, feeling her breasts rise.

His eyes feast on her full, supple shape. "Beautiful."

Kissing her neck, his hand gently touches her nipple, igniting the detonation of tiny fireworks all over her body. He cups her breast, licks her nipples, alternating between gently kissing, caressing, sucking and dragging his teeth around the erect nodes. Playfully feeding into her fantasy. She feels the heat rising in her thighs. Longing, wet and delicious. The moisture seeps between her thighs.

Then his lips travel down her stomach, taking his time to explore and taste her warm skin. He unzips her slacks, she steps out of the puddle it forms around her feet.

Brian traces the line left by her lingerie with his mouth, biting at the strings until his mouth finds her mound. He removes her underwear, kissing her above her pubic bone.

"You make me weak," she reiterates.

He turns her around, admiring her femininity. Jordan is very complaisant with all her clothes off. She moves readily to his touch. She's gorgeous. Slim. A Brazilian strip of light hair leads down between her legs. "Just look at you, you gorgeous woman." She smiles when he kisses her.

"I love kissing your smile," he says, which makes her smile more and so he kisses her again.

Her hands move to feel him, hard and horny.

Jordan unbuckles his belt and pushes her hands over his firm buttocks, forcing his pants down. He is not wearing underwear. His erect flesh appears, shaven and circumcised. There's decent girth and length to satisfy a woman.

She pecks at his nipple, her hand descending, finding his testicles first. She curls her fingers around his bristling flesh, drawing her fingers across its underside. An intricate science, his whole being contained there, like a ship in a bottle.

She loves the way his body responds to her touch, the way he catches his breath as she moves her hand until she arrives at the base of his penis, which she holds with extreme care, attempting to gauge how sensitive or robust it is.

She breaks the kiss to look down. A pearl of pre-cum forms on the swollen head of his cock.

I want him inside of me.

Her fingers trail along its length, noting its silky texture, until she feels the throbbing tip, which she lightly strokes, and then, she firmly adjusts his cock back and downwards until she feels it just touching her labia. Standing at her door.

Jordan lies down, stretching like a cat. Brian removes his socks and slides over her. He takes possession of her. Urgent, long and slow kisses, slipping her hands above her head, tasting her lips, her mouth, her tongue.

She enjoys his weight on her, being pinned under his body. She wants him soldered to her, from mouth to feet.

He flicks her nipples with his tongue. She feels her nipples perk, sensitive pebbles. His mouth cups the fleshy place where her rib cage softens into her breast, nipping at her smooth, white dunes. Slow, rhythmic, gentle bites, moving down her body, to her navel, sending sweet spasms through her. She grabs his hair, panting as she feels his warm breath on her mound. Her pelvis rises, spreads, like a bowl offering up succulent red fruit. He nuzzles her softly around the vulva, his beard is a little rough on the insides of her thighs.

Then with his tongue, he strikes fire, pushing into her.

She cries out in wonderment, almost in gratitude at being touched in the right places. Again he plunders her with his tongue, setting off another melodious moan. He plays her sensual instrument, evoking the most glorious sounds. Delicious notes of pleasure.

"Is this beautiful to you?" she gasps.

"Oh yes," he replies, "you glisten."

His hands cup both her breasts. He kisses her, full on her tumescent lips, gently, then with increasing pressure he follows with his tongue, barely touching her clitoris as he moves up and down the erectile organ.

Every lick sends a pulsating wave of pleasure through her being. He squeezes hard on her nipples.

Fuck!

She fantasizes about taking his rock-hard cock in her mouth, tasting him, cupping his balls with one hand, and stroking his girth with the other until her chin is dripping wet and he is on the verge of exploding.

I'm going to cum!

Jordan grabs at him desperately, pressing his warm mouth hard against her soft moist folds, wanting him to stop, bucking her hips, not wanting him to stop. She pulls his face up to hers. Brian's weight rests on his elbows and forearms, planted on either side of her head. The sum of small acts unite them, the mathematics of desire. She wants to thrust him deep inside her, to watch his face as he penetrates her. She wants his sweat to drop onto her. She wants to leave her drops on him.

Her thighs are wet, warm and inviting. Her breath is short. His prick is hard, pressing against her labia.

"God, you are beautiful." His voice is barely audible.

"I want you inside me."

She moves to guide him into her. He gently takes her hand in his, adjusts his hips until she can feel the mild pressure of his cock lightly pushing her folds aside, as he gently enters her. She lets out a deep sigh, closes her eyes, throws her head back and grabs the sheets.

Brian slides deeper into her, filling her up. She feels his cock pressing against her cervix. His hips remain motionless, keeping the pressure down while he passionately kisses her open mouth.

This is how people die!

Jordan quivers with pleasure, a hoarse moan escapes her as she reaches climax. Her legs clench down on Brian's hips as she cums in waves. Her head thrown back.

Brian watches in admiration at the splendor of the female orgasm. He waits, tranquil, deliberate.

She releases her grip, her eyelids flutter. She swims up to the surface of consciousness. Her flesh is innocent and warm.

Jordan's blonde hair lies sprawled around her face. Her eyes are closed and her lips are stretched in an involuntary smile. A holy representation of Venus.

Brian begins a slow rotation of his hips. Gliding in and out of her in long, delicious moves. Her hands swim down along her flanks, rubbing her hips. She slips her right hand down between his groin and hers. He lifts a little to let her through. She places her fingers around his lubricated shaft, putting pressure on her clitoris, as he pulls out and enters her again and again.

The sensation on her G-spot becomes unbearable as he picks up the tempo, repeatedly jabbing and bumping into her. He pulls out.

"Stop baby. I'm going to squirt!"

He plunges into her. She cums again. Jordan grabs onto him until the ripples of ecstasy subside.

Brian smiles. "That's good to know."

"I don't want to wet your bed."

Brian hooks his knees outside her legs and drives himself deeper. She is warm, wet, and inviting. "Oh god," she breathes, "that's the best."

Brian's kiss is urgent, his pelvic bone stimulates her clitoris with every push.

"I want you to cum with me," Jordan whispers in his ear. Brian pulls her along to the edge of sensation and then lets her pull back ever so gently.

"I want to see you cum."

Jordan is ready to dive again. She feels the taut, sure strength in his hips as he presses into her, forcing her to press back. Back and forth and back and forth. She offers no resistance.

She cums in long, trembling runs. His muscular back arches in spasms as he empties himself over her in gouts, in vigorous but diminishing quantities, filling her navel and coating her belly in a tepid, viscous fluid.

She grabs him and directs him inside her.

"Stay inside me." Brian complies. He kisses her smiles.

-SIXTY-TWO-

†

Bethelsdorp, typically a vibrant suburb, tonight dons an unusual hush. The streets, usually abuzz with activity, stand deserted under the tyranny of a thunderous downfall. Raindrops play a percussive symphony, drowning out the usual hum of urban life.

Iggi's black VW rolls down the narrow lanes toward his modest single-story house. In the torrential cascade, the exterior of his residence appears nondescript and indistinguishable from its neighbors. Brick buildings, low fences crafted from ready-made concrete slabs, manually operated gates, and corrugated garage doors- all the familiar elements of suburban uniformity. The intentional lack of ostentation is a silent pact with the neighborhood- a commitment to blending in.

Here, you don't bring the Maserati home; it remains confined to the dealership or perhaps your lavish Camps Bay abode. It's a coded language spoken among those in the know; a subtle art of status and discretion. Diplomatic

camouflage and Iggi understands it well. The comrades and cadres, like him, have mastered the art of appearing unremarkable in their immediate surroundings. It's a calculated move, a strategic choice to navigate the delicate dance of power and influence.

A Golf GTI is an acceptable insignia. Your basic bling. Understanding the first commandment is what makes Iggi the undisputed Lord of this borough which is known as a hotbed of rebellious behavior by the Khoi-khoi.

You may operate a savage syndicate in exchange for anonymity and immunity, just as long as you share in the community through job creation and selective philanthropy.

Because he did not germinate from Bethelsdorp earth, his financial aid to the political coffers, confers Iggi his status. Or maybe it's just the manner in which he holds the Glock 9mm when he speaks to someone, that gets his message through.

He ascended the ranks of the order, because he kept their commandments. He worked the streets, held his peace, did his time and he pays his bills but not his taxes. Cash is king. And he is a kingmaker.

Iggi guides the black VW to a halt in front of his garage, the drumming rain challenging him to step into its pelting embrace.

He sits for a moment, gathering the courage to face the storm that awaits beyond the car doors. Raindrops smatter against the windscreen in a relentless rhythm. The wipers engage in a choreographed Samba, effortlessly volleying every raindrop away. Tiny rivers race down the side panes, tracing ephemeral paths on the glass.

The world beyond the car is blurred, distorted by the cascading water, and there's a serene beauty in the eye of the storm. Amber light spills from the steamy kitchen window, casting an inviting glow that transforms raindrops on the glass into effervescent jewels. From the kitchen emanates the comforting aroma of West African cuisine.

Iggi sprints for the garage door, hoists it up, and waits inside as if a better opportunity will present itself or that the rain will cease and allow him dry passage back to the vehicle.

A transverse bolt illuminates the skyline, and rolling thunder follows suit. "Jeesis!" He exclaims, his heart pounding in sync with the violent rhythm of the storm. The deafening echoes of thunder linger.

Iggi attempts to regain his visual perception, placing his palms over his eyes. He holds and releases, hoping to dispel the disorientation.

As the world slowly comes back to center, Iggi squints to focus. There, next to the hood of a parked car, stands the figment of a man, clad in a Macintosh that billows like a phantom cloak. Iggi, accustomed to a longer-than-usual glare recovery time, narrows his eyes, trying to discern the details in the obscured silhouette. Time's up.

The first projectile rips into Iggi's eye socket. He dies where he stands. His dark life is extinguished in an instant.

The stranger moves closer, unfazed by the gruesome tableau. The following two rounds are fired with chilling intent, aimed not at random but at vital organs. Each shot is a cold, methodical execution, punctuating the storm's crescendo with the staccato rhythm of a lethal symphony. The thunder and rain conspire to erase the traces of the salvo, as if nature itself were complicit in this clandestine act. With calculated intent, the gunman collects the spent 9mm casings, a silent acknowledgment of a job done.

Tonight becomes the night that Iggi brought the inevitable thunder home.

-SIXTY-THREE-

†

Last night's torrid baptism cleansed the battalion of Spire roses and the beds of Hybrid tea roses that grace Petronella's garden. The morning unfolds with a sense of renewal, the air crisp and laden with the intoxicating blend of fruit and honey emanating from the Iceberg rose bushes.

Petronella's hands move with practiced grace, collecting a tray adorned with delicate china cups and a steaming teapot. She carries this offering of solace to the lounge, where her guests, Jordan, David, and Cheryl, sit in quiet communion with the past. The family album, a cherished relic of shared history, lies open before them. Its pages tell stories in faded photographs, capturing moments of joy, sorrow, and the inexorable passage of time.

Jordan and Cheryl, entranced by the visual narrative, momentarily cease their journey through the familial tapestry when Petronella enters.

As she places the tray on the table, the air becomes infused with the fragrant dance of brewing tea leaves.

"Should I pour?" she asks.

"Thank you." They reply as a choir.

Petronella pours perfectly steeped Earl Grey into Royal Albert cups. The delicate clink of cups meeting saucers resonates in the room. The delicate floral patterns on the set release a reel of memories in the siblings. Jordan's eyes well up, and when she makes contact with her brother, she finds his eyes are drowning as well.

They both let out a bout of laughter, amused by their shared moment of silly nostalgia. Cheryl pouts in compassion.

Petronella is oblivious to the situation. "Please add milk to your taste," she says, offering a scone to Cheryl.

"I am fine, thank you," Cheryl declines, then she dives right in.

"What was Stewart like as a boy?"

"Oh, he was a rumbustious child. Very temperamental. Always fighting with his brother."

"You already had a son, when you adopted Stewart?"

Petronella points to a black-and-white picture of a young man in a navy uniform. "Yes. He is a year older than Stewart. Stewie would bite me, his teachers, the children, everyone. And when I locked him in his room, he would break down the place. Then I had to put him in a cupboard. He is a wild one."

"What was the relationship between your husband and Stewart like?"

"He could control the boy but when he passed away I felt that I could not cope with such a difficult child. He had to go to Protea House."

"And did that help?"

"Not really. He was always making up these outrageous stories of the people there. He assaulted a boy there as well, if I can remember well."

Jordan points to a photo of Stewart in an Army uniform. "And then he did military service?"

"Only four months. He tried to commit suicide so they discharged him. I moved here to Despatch and he came to stay with me. Then he met Lynn, Lynn Havenga."

"Lynn was his first wife?"

"Yes, she is the mother of Wuané."

Petronella pages to a photo of an eleven-year-old girl. Wuane's dark hair is styled in a boy's cut. "You can take that picture. The newspapers made a print copy."

Jordan removes the photo from the album. "Do you know where Wuané could be?"

"Veronica is hiding her, I am certain. She always defends him. She is his girlfriend or whatever-"

"Thank you, we'll talk to her as well," David states as he gets up to leave.

Petronella hands a torn box to Jordan. "Here are some more photos and old films of Stewart from when he was young. You can keep them."

Cheryl's phone rings. She walks outside to answer. The others follow as Petronella escorts them to the gate.

"I cannot believe that Stewart keeps on hurting people. Such a disappointment. I don't know where he went wrong."

As they get into the vehicle, Cheryl ends her phone conversation. She turns to David. "Another boy has gone missing. Benjamin Mathews."

"When did he go missing?" Jordan asks.

"Two days ago."

"Then he may still be linked to Stewart," David adds.

Cheryl agrees and reminds him, "We still have an interview with Lynn Havenga later today"

"Fuck it yes! Four-thirty." David says as he fires up the engine and speaks to Jordan via the rear view mirror. "Let's go talk to Stewie. Maybe he'll tell you where to find Benjamin."

-SIXTY-FOUR-

†

Stewart finishes a sandwich. He licks a last smidgen of mustard sauce from the polystyrene tray, burps and drags a sleeve across his greasy mouth. He leans back, waiting for Jordan's attention. His demeanor is that of the teacher's pet in the front row of a class, eager to please yet harboring an undercurrent of defiance.

Cheryl starts the camera with a *ping* that resonates in the hushed atmosphere. The room turns from a cafeteria back into a theater of investigation once more, and the suspect, a willing thespian in the drama he aim to direct.

Jordan, expecting David to kick off the inquisition with a pertinent question, is met with a surprising twist. Instead, he spurs her on with a simple nod. It's a silent acknowledgment that the moment has arrived; the spotlight is hers.

Is death this woman's mate?

"What do you want to tell me today?"

"And you wanted to talk about when I was a boy."

"Yes. Tell me about your step-parents. Were they kind to you?

"Daddy was okay. And Petronella punished me a lot."

"Why did she punish you?"

"And she was angry for what happened at school. She locked me up in the cupboard when I walked in my sleep."

"How old were you then?"

"I think six, seven. And when I pissed in my bed- She put me in baths of very cold water." Jordan takes down notes as he speaks.

Lock in small spaces. Isolated. Bed-wetter.

162

"What did your father say?"

"He tried and then he died. And then she put me in Protea Hill."

"Protea Hill reformatory?"

"And because I bit the teacher," Steward adds.

"I am sorry about your father, Stewart. Why did you bite the teacher?"

"Other boys bullied and mocked me, so, and then I kicked one in the balls. And she came and hit me. And I bit the fucking bitch! On her tits," he chuckles, "and on her arms and legs. And the principal grabbed my hair and he and beat me with a cane in front of everybody."

"What did your mother do?"

"Petronella? Nothing. She tied my hands to the bed and beat me till I pissed and shat myself. She said I must stop biting. And she locked me in my room and I said to myself that I would be my own mother and father and sister and auntie and fuck God and fuck everybody!" Stewart screams, putting everyone on edge.

Silence.

Jordan is the first to speak again. "Tell me about the reformatory."

"And it's not a reform school," Stewart laughs, "and it is a fucking prison for children and some big kids were there because they stabbed their mothers and so there are gangs and big boys that have been to prison for long before they go there. And they look at you, and you know-." He shakes his head violently. "And the teachers let the older boys lock us up at night so that we can't run away. But then, when it was dark and then those- And you hear them, the watchers, the torturers, sneaking in,- but you can't see; it's too dark and they start choosing a young boy to rape and you can hear how they hold him and how they all fuck him. You can hear how they slap against him and they laugh. Sometimes it is quick, and sometimes it takes a long tine and we can't sleep when they take long. And the next day that boy cries all day at school and the teacher smacks him for crying and we can say nothing to him. And then sometimes, they come for me and take my clothes off, and if you fight, they hit you, and then those big boys hold me down, and then they rape me, and when one cums on you, the next boy fuck you until they all cum. And you smell like cum all night. And the next day you are crying-And nobody can say nothing to you."

It's moments like these that Jordan feels the weight of her own inadequacy, a profound sense of powerlessness in the face of the twisted depravity that lies within the human form. She grapples with the harsh truth that there are depths of darkness she may never fully comprehend. It takes a moment- a pregnant pause in the flow of time, for her to summon the strength to respond.

"Why didn't you report it?"

"You can't snitch. Fuck, you will be knifed! Or they say you fell in the shower. You just get fucked when it's your turn. And you get used to it until new boys come in. And then even at that church. The deacon from Mom's church, and he saw me smoking marijuana. And he took me to his house. And he told me to lie over his table. I thought he was going to hit me. And he put his dry cock in me. He fucks a lot of boys, that man of God."

Jordan opens her mouth, but she isn't able to utter a sound. The synapses between the mind and the voice have lost connection. She feels the weight of responsibility pressing down on her shoulders. The echoes of the depravity she is witnessing, reverberates in her mind, creating a malevolent crescendo that lingers.

"But I have learned from my beatings," Stewart continues, "and the next time he wanted to rape me, I pissed myself and shit on his cock. And didn't want to touch me again."

The room, suffused with an unsettling silence, becomes a suffocating shroud. Eventually, David asks, "Do you become violent when you smoke marijuana?"

"With Mandrax in- And I am going to stop that, and that's why I hurt that boy for fucking."

"How do you hurt them?" David asks.

Jordan finds her voice. "Wait, which boy are you talking about?"

A dire shadow draws across Stewart's hardwood eyes. Compelled by a force beyond his control, his movements become deliberate, each gesture a calculated movement. He leans back.

"That boy. I fucked him before you came to take me from the boat."

"You had sex with the boy on that same morning? Is his name Benjamin?"

Stewart becomes both storyteller and character, navigating the twisted corridors of his own creation. "I see a lot of them at night- dead, and I can see how they go to God. I put my hands or something around the neck, and then I squeeze harder and harder, and then I fuck until they make that jelly bean- effect. And that makes me cum." Stewart rubs over his groin.

Her stomach churns, still, Jordan gives nothing away.

"Jelly bean effect?"

"When their eyes open up and their lips are blue- How can I say it? When we fuck. It's when I squeeze and their tongues swell up and their lips and eyes bulge and pop like jelly beans."

Stewart's hand goes into his pocket, and he rubs himself. He is detached from his environment. It's like he's seeing straight through Jordan. "And I wait for their jelly beans, and that makes me cum, a lot-"

Stewart jumps up. "And I need to go to piss now!" A police officer removes him.

The air remains thick with a palpable revolt. Jordan's breath comes in ragged gasps, each inhale a struggle against the invisible weight pressing down on her chest. Her heartbeat echoes in her ears, a rapid drumming that threatens to drown out reason.

She grips the sides of her chair, her knuckles turning white as she fights to maintain control. A sharp pang shoots through her temple, a searing pain that makes her wince. Fear courses through her veins like wildfire. Panic.

Is it a stroke?

Jordan's head drops slowly, almost involuntarily, as if the weight of the world is pulling her down. In a sudden burst of adrenaline, Jordan jerks her head up, her eyes wide with determination.

With a sharp inhale, she pushes herself away from the desk, the chair scraping against the floor as she rises.

The office door beckons like a lifeline, an escape route from the impending doom.

Fuck the Mariner!

Jordan storms out, her hurried footsteps echoing in the corridor.

-SIXTY-FIVE-

†

When Brian eventually catches up with Jordan, she is halfway across a rugby field, chasing off to nowhere. His voice slices through the air, a sharp command that echoes against the vastness of the field. "Stop!" he calls out, the word hanging in the tension between them.

Jordan slows, her footsteps faltering but not halting completely. The wind tousles her blonde hair, and she turns to face Brian with a defiant glint in her eyes.

"Where are you going?" Brian demands, breathless from the chase, his words carrying a sense of urgency and confusion. Her response is a mixture of defiance and vulnerability, a silent plea for understanding that lingers in the charged atmosphere.

"I don't know," she admits, her voice carried away by the wind. Brian takes a step closer, the gap narrowing but the emotional distance between them remains.

"This guy is beyond fucked-up! He gets aroused when talking about assaulting and murdering children!"

Brian reaches out, but she pulls away and is on the move again. Brian battles to keep up. "Where are you going?"

"He is fucking masturbating in there right now!" The world holds its breath as if anticipating the revelation of a profound secret, hidden within the depths of Jordan's untamed spirit.

"I need some time- Fuck! I can't do this. Leave me." Brian gropes for words.

"Go!"

Jordan darts straight towards the rugby club.

The clubhouse, a shadowy enclave tucked away in the heart of the city, is a haven for the solitary and the familiar faces of the neighborhood.

Dimly lit, with a faint hum of conversation and the distant roar of a rugby match on a battered television, it's a place where secrets are exchanged over cheap drinks and the worn upholstery of well-worn bar stools.

Jordan pushes through the creaking door, stepping into the murky ambiance that clings to the air. The club is surprisingly alive for this time of day, a fact that catches her off guard. A quick glance at her watch reveals the reason for the unexpected crowd.

Oh! It's lunchtime.

Navigating through a wank of horny toads leering at every woman who dares to step inside, Jordan weaves her way towards the bar.

"Gin and tonic, please," she orders, her voice cutting through the low murmur of conversations and the clink of glasses. As the bartender sets to work, Jordan catches her reflection in the warped mirror beyond the counter. Her image, distorted and fragmented. Her reflection mirrors the fractured reality of the club itself.

She studies the rabble of patrons, a collection of mismatched souls with stories etched into the lines on their faces and the stains on their worn clothing.

She mumbles to herself. "The Wedding Guest he beat his breast, yet he cannot choose but hear; and thus spake on that ancient man, the bright-eyed Mariner- and the rest of the world is out, fucking drinking!"

The bartender, not convinced that he's serving the actual famous author, whose name he can't remember, plants a pink drink in front of Jordan. She checks the slip and pays in cash.

"Thanks."

She takes a moment to savor the concoction's bitterness before glancing at the ornate mirror again. A smirk plays on her lips; she appreciates the energy, revels in it. But then, she catches a glimpse in the mirror that sends a shiver down her spine. Her jade eyes widen as she locks onto the reflection. There, amid the wreckage, stands the tall man; that shadowy figure with ill intent.

A chill races through her veins. The unsettling realization grips her: he's watching, lurking in the periphery. The uneasy feeling intensifies, a cloak of paranoia settling over her like a suffocating fog. Every nerve in her body screams a warning. The crowd becomes a blur, and her focus narrows to the sinister silhouette in the mirror.

"Fuck this," she growls, slamming the glass down. She takes a deep, steadying breath, tasting the metallic tang of fear. With resolve hardening her gaze, she spins around, ready to confront the looming threat. But he's gone. A sharp curse escapes her lips, frustration and anxiety intertwining.

"Fuck!"

She pushes through the sea of bodies, navigating the maze of pulsating lights and dancing shadows, scanning the room, searching for any trace of the tall man.

As she reaches the entrance, the heavy door swings open with a creak. The night air rushes in, carrying a bitter chill.

Vanished!

-SIXTY-SIX-

†

Two stoic officers, their uniforms crisply pressed, guard the entrance to the room where the Mariner sits in ominous silence. As the distant echo of heels against linoleum grows louder, the anticipation morphs into an uneasy tension.

Click-clack, click-clack!

The rhythmic cadence foreshadows the impending arrival of Jordan. The corridor, a sterile artery of the building, reverberates with each step, a warning drum-roll to the imminent storm. And then she appears- a force of nature in human form.

Jordan barrels down the narrow passage with a determination that rivals that of a Pamplona bull charging through the cobbled streets. Her presence is felt before she is seen, a whirlwind of energy evading bystanders like a seasoned matador navigating a chaotic arena. The onlookers, both those familiar with her glamour and those encountering her unadorned face for the first time, share a moment of disbelief. The woman before them, once radiant and formidable, now bears the marks of a loss that transcends mere physical appearance. It's not just the absence of makeup; it's the dimming of a once-glowing spirit.

I must look like shit.

David lets out an "Aleluya!" when he spots his sister. "He refuses to talk to anyone but you."

Jordan ignores his statement. "He is not working alone," she says to Brian.

"Why do you think that?".

"Remember the man I showed you in the photograph?"

Brian nods. "The blurred image, yes?"

"He is the one stalking me."

"Are you sure?"

"I'll prove it to you."

Jordan collects herself, straightens her black suit and enters the office. Stewart stops his discussion with Griebenow mid-sentence and applauds Jordan's return to the arena. "Hey, you're back!"

Jordan is in no mood for pleasantries. She pulls her chair closer while the others scramble to find their positions.

Cheryl gets the camera going just in time to capture Jordan's first question.

"Why do you think that you get to send people to God?" Her tone borders on sarcasm.

Stewart is caught off guard. "Because they didn't have it good and they are meek- don't you think it's better to be with Jesus? What will you do when someone you love is suffering and you don't have your money and your child has no food and people hit your child and rape your child. Must we die slowly so you can feel better?"

"You are not God."

"I don't keep their souls."

"I can't think now-" It take time for Jordan to get up. She moves behind her chair before her parched voice breaks through.

"Stewart, you said that you killed many people, and so far you have only told me about five boys-"

"But you said you wanted to talk about the boys."

"Mister Wilken-" Griebenow interjects.

Stewart doesn't pay heed to his councilor.

"Do you want me to tell you about the whores?" Steward whispers. "Okay, I will take you to all the whores so that you can see that I'm Boetie Boer," he growls.

Then his demeanor changes in an instant. "But I am too hungry now. You were late." Stewart turns to David. "Can we get hamburgers again?"

Jordan shoots Brian a glance. His train of thought is traveling between the stations of stupefied and ecstatic.

"Wait!" Jordan exclaims. "Do you mean to tell me that you killed women as well?"

"Just whores. Women who sell their cunts for money and for what God has given them for free. That's stealing!"

The wall on the beach!

"And you were there. I saw you and you saw what I did when I cut that slut." Jordan grips the back of her chair. "Yes, I want to ask you about that day-"

Stewart jumps up. "I'm going to eat first. All this talking makes me hungry."

He jumps up and walks out. The officers flank Stewart down the long corridor of the precinct, each step reverberates with the heavy clank of shackles at his feet. A flickering fluorescent light cast an eerie green tinge along the corridor, amplifying the sense of foreboding that permeates the air.

As they reach the end of the corridor, Stewart casts one last glance over his shoulder as if he could feel Jordan's gaze upon him.

-SIXTY-SEVEN-

†

Alone, alone, all, all alone,
Alone on a wide wide sea!
And never a saint took pity on
My soul in agony.
- The Rime of the Ancient Mariner

IN THIS FORGOTTEN CORNER of Relton Street, where alcohol reigns supreme and paint is a luxury, Jordan finds herself immersed in a world where resilience and despair coexist.

There is a desperate plea for attention from most buildings, and Lynn Havenga's place is one of them. A relic of neglect amidst the chaos of a neighborhood ensnared by decay. Most of the outer wall is chipped away, exposing concrete and red brick pillars on the porch, which forms part of the front yard. There is no space for a lawn. Once you step off the pavement, you are on the front stoop.

David finds parking right in front of the porch. Jordan spots a red car in the driveway. It's hoisted up, resting on four stacks of bricks. A symbol of unrealized aspirations, suspended in time like the dreams of its owner.

Ironically, the neighbor's yard is crammed with vehicles under repair, the air thick with the acrid scent of paint
thinner and the distant hum of power tools.

The front door, once a vibrant color that now fades to a dreary gray, stands slightly ajar, as if reluctant to welcome any visitors. David knocks, and the hinges protest with a screech that reverberates through the empty foyer.

Cheryl introduces the gang to Lynn when she eventually shows up to lead them into the lounge. Inside, the air is heavy with the musty scent of dust. Glaring light filters through cracked blinds, casting contrasting lines across the threadbare carpet. Lynn Havenga's life, like the peeling layers of paint on her walls, is exposed to anyone who cares to look.

In the living room, an assortment of mismatched furniture creates a haphazard mosaic. A worn-out couch sags under the weight of forgotten dreams, and a coffee table, scarred with countless rings from neglected cups, sits as a silent witness to the passage of time. And nailed to a wall is the newspaper report of Wuané's disappearance. It has been neatly cut out and framed.

This is Wuane's world.

Jordan still can't disengage from Stewart's statements and finds it hard to concentrate. Cheryl however, doesn't waste time. She shoots from the hip.

"How did you meet Stewart."

"We met at a nightclub. I liked to dance- He was so shy. But I became pregnant with Wuané. Look, he was a good man in the beginning, but when he smokes himself moff- stupid, then he is a monster. He would beat us."

"You and your children?"

"Oh ja. Me, my daughter and then Wuané was born. Then he wanted only to have sex-round the back. I didn't want to, it was sore."

"Sorry."

Lynn scoffs. "Sometimes, I had to go and sex a guy to buy food for us, then he became very jealous. Once he wanted to shot a policeman who was here. The cop paid double to naai here! He called me a slut when we fight. Then he goes to the whores and blames me." She lights a cigarette.

"So many times I called the police and the girls would cry, when they came they took him for Marijuana. Then he would come and beat me again."

"Then you divorced him and married again?"

"Yes. When we got divorced, Stewart said he would never have sex with a white woman again."

Lynn's husband brings her a glass of water and a hand full of pills. Lynn scoffs them down. "Dankie," she thanks him as he leaves the room. Cheryl continues, "Did he say why?"

"Because it might be his missing sister," she laughs. "Lekker crazy! He hates sluts who give sex for money because of me, but he was always with the whores. If he had money, he would be smoking and whoring."

"What do you think happened to Wuané?"

"No. He hides her. He says we cannot feed her. He wanted to take her, then I called the police. That was with my second husband, I do not want him close to her. Because he gets violent when he smokes."

"And now you are married to your third husband?"

Lynn chortles. "Yes. I am becoming like Elizabeth Taylor."

Jordan is too set on getting out, to fake a smile. "Do you think he would hurt her?"

"No. Maybe. He always comes here and makes trouble. He told everyone that we were molesting her, you see. But it was kak! Wuané loves him. Always together. He's hiding her with someone." Lynn's distress is palpable.

She reaches for a glass of water, her trembling hands betraying the turmoil within. "A mother wants to know."

"I can understand, and that's why we are here. Where do you think he would keep her?" Jordan's question hangs in the air, a plea for a lifeline.

Lynn springs up, agitated, as if the mere thought sends shivers down her spine. "I don't know. Jeesis, I am too scared to think about it, maybe on a boat or an island. You must go now. Find my Wuané. Please bring her home."

The urgency in Lynn's plea propels them into action. She storms off, leaving the trio to see themselves out.

-SIXTY-EIGHT-

†

B rian starts dishing up as soon as Jordan enters the lounge. The aroma of exotic spices fills the air. "Your biryani smells delicious," she remarks.

Wearing Brian's black fleece gown and slippers, Jordan is still drying her hair with a towel, which she casually hangs over the back of a chair before taking a seat on the couch. Two glasses of wine are waiting patiently for them on the coffee table. Brian joins her, placing their meals before her. "Dinner is served."

"Are there any Islands close to shore?" she inquires.

Brian hands her a glass of wine and settles close to her on the couch. "There are three rocky islands just off the coast: St. Croix, Brenton, and Jahleel. But you can't go there, obviously; it's not open to the public. It's an established breeding ground for the jackass penguins. Why do you want to know?"

Jordan takes a sip of her wine, her gaze contemplative.

"But someone with a boat can reach them?"

"Only St Croix is large enough to house a governmental structure. It's a reserve and it's patrolled. Why?"

"So there isn't a possibility of Wuané being kept on one of the Islands?"

"I'll check, but it's highly unlikely that the scientists would allow it. They would report it immediately, I'm sure."

"It's just something that Lynn said today that made me wonder. I feel like a chameleon inside a box of M&M's. I don't know which freaking color to turn into, to retain my sanity."

"His profile floored me as well. Targeting both boys and women and different races? A paedophile plus a necrophile?"

Jordan shivers, "Let's not talk shop at all tonight. Let's watch something."

"I concur."

Brian puts the TV on. They enjoy the meal while watching a program in silence. Then Jordan collects the dishes to take to the kitchen.

"I am sorry for this afternoon- I lost it. Again."

"I understand completely. It is not fair towards you and Cheryl, for that matter."

"Thank you for understanding."

"But I want to ask you something?"

"What is it?"

"What do you need, Jade?"

"What I need may not be what I want," she answers, "what I need is to be vulnerable, to feel anxious about losing someone like you. But what I want is not to feel defenseless because it scares me. There is an element of rejection associated with loss. Without vulnerability there is no love. It's the age old struggle between the head and the heart."

"I have nowhere else to be."

"Thank you for understanding."

"Thank you, for touching me with your wonderful soul," Brian whispers.

She places their bowls on the table and moves onto his lap. "That is beautiful! I believe I'll need a kiss to go with those words."

She uses her thumb to tilt his face, the other fingers splayed behind his ear, into his hair.

Intimacy, adequate intimacy.

Jordan takes charge and he likes it. His head rolls to the side. She cups his jaw and looks down at him. A burst of emotions expand inside of her. He sees it and smiles. "Hell baby, take all the kisses you need." And so she does.

She pulls his shirt over his head and clumps it around his wrists, holding his hands down. She pushes his naked torso back against the couch and kisses his chest, moving down to his navel. She lifts herself sufficiently to remove his shorts, admiring his male physique.

She opens her robe just enough to reveal a succulent slice of the sweetmeats he is about to be served. She straddles his groin, her clitoris caressing his shaft, her wet folds slipping on his erection. She draws her hair around them like a tent.

"I can't get enough of your hair," Brian smiles, drawing it over her shoulders. "The way it curls around my fingers like it's alive. I can't get enough of your hair, I can't get enough of you."

Jordan drags her hair across his face, letting her tits touch his mouth. Her nipples are hard. She kisses him, wet, wicked kisses. Brian attempts to get as much of her breasts into his mouth as possible, sinking his teeth into her fleshiest parts.

Jordan drops the robe, serving him the full portion.

She uses her hand to slip Brian inside her. He drives himself harder into her. She positions the bulb of his cock against her G-spot.

Jordan rocks back and forth until things get all twisted and hot inside. She clenches and unclenches, siphoning all the ecstasy from her body. She can discern the emotions inside Brian. She feels them slowly working their way through his organ, into her. It's the most unexpected sensation, more intimate than simple sexual gratification.

A current tugging at her, moving her towards a flood.

"I want you to cum with me," she pants.

Brian squeezes her firm butt, his middle finger probes her round ass, then with the tip, he massages her stretched sphincter. She opens her mouth, unable to utter a sound.

The tide rises into an unstoppable wave. She feels all of him pass into her.

"I'm going to cum!" The moan that finds its way out of her throat, is downright sinful. He wants to hear it over and over again, he wants his touch to be the only one that could elicit that pleasure.

She puts her mouth on his. His fingers pull her hair back like torn silk. He watches her face as he ejaculates inside her. Lubricating her walls with warm juice, then her body, erupts into ringing, like a bell tower where the fryer is swinging madly on the rope.

-SIXTY-NINE-

†

Jordan sits doodling and grinning like an idiot, her eyes fixated on the paper as her hand moves effortlessly, the pen an extension of her thoughts. A grin, infectious and genuine, stretches across her face, giving life to the doodles that dance beneath the pen's strokes.

In the corner, Cheryl, with a mischievous twinkle in her eyes, quietly captures the moment on film. Jordan, lost in her world of doodles, remains oblivious to the invisible lens that has captured the raw essence of her emotions.

Her bubble pops when Cheryl asks. "Anything you wish to share?"

A blush tinges her cheeks, but the glow of bliss remains.

"It was incredible, but you can't coax any more detail out of me."

"You sure?" Cheryl checks.

"Just don't try this at home."

"That good?"

Jordan grins and nods. Cheryl smirks, satisfied with the tease, and strides back to her camera with a playful twirl.

As Brian enters the room, he's greeted with Cheryl's 'pouted lips look,' a non-verbal cue that speaks volumes. He chuckles, easily picking up on the unspoken language.

Girl talk.

David, immersed in his own world of business, remains oblivious to the lighthearted exchange. Stewart, followed by his lawyer, struts in and greets Jordan like he's a sportscaster psyched for a big game. "And how was your weekend, Jordan?"

"Good, thank you. How was yours?" Jordan throws the line like a skilled thespian.

"Fucking arresting!" Stewart busts a nut, and Jordan fakes a smile. She produces a photograph from the file and holds it up, while she studies Stewart's face. It's the photo of Benjamin Mathews. Stewart studies the boy. Jordan can't detect a response. She sighs. "In fact, Stewart, my weekend was not good at all. I can't write."

"Why not?"

"Because Benjamin Mathews is somewhere out there, and I can't write a word, when my mind is preoccupied with the whereabouts of Harry and Wuané. Can you help me?"

"Maybe they are at the house?"

There is a silent beat before Jordan responds. "Which house are you referring to, Stewart?" The penny drops.

"You got someone to call us?"

Stewart realizes his mistake. "No!"

"You are not operating alone. How many are you?" Jordan gets in Stewart's face. "Your girlfriend! She made the call! It was a ploy, to make us believe that Harry was abducted as a sex worker."

"Jordan, I-"

"You deceived me. You said that if I listen, you'll tell me the truth. Where is our respect?" She packs her stuff.

"It was her plan, not mine." Stewart stutters.

"When was the last time that you saw Harry?"

"The morning before you arrested me?"

Stewart's answer hits Jordan in the gut. "What? Where?"

"I told you, I sexed him." That one lands on the solar plexus. "Stewart. Is Harry alive?"

He shakes his head. "I'll show you where I put Harry."

It's a hollow victory. Jordan slumps into her chair, arms flaccid. A defeated fighter who never expected to get beaten. Brian moves to put his hands on her deflated shoulders. David places a satellite map on the desk in front of Stewart, who struggles at first to find his bearings.

"Where?"

"Where are the salt pans?"

David points to the landmark on the map. "Here."

Stewart leans over the map. "And Algoa Park?"

"Here."

"Then we walked this way-"

"Along Dyke Road?" Stewart nods. He struggles to point out his route with both hands cuffed. "Behind these flats, then we went into the field here-"

"Where people dump their rubbish?" David asks.

"Yes. Yes, here. Here he is."

David dashes out of his office, taking the map with him. CSI needs to get cracking. A hefty atmosphere perforates the room. "But I don't know this boy," Stewart mutters, pointing at the photo of Benjamin.

Before Jordan can respond, Griebenow puts a stop to her line of questioning. Jordan leans forward, she takes pensive sips from her soda, then grits her teeth, sending her muscle memory receptors to find the file marked *Drama class, 2nd-year university.*

"Thank you for bringing Harry home to his mother." She delivers her line, unrehearsed, persuasive. Stewart finds it credible.

"Harry is my friend. And he ran away from that house because that man kicked him and he was very sad and he is now in a good place."

Jordan disregards Stewart's explanation, her focus unwavering. "You wanted to tell me about the women as well?" Her tone is both assertive and curious, a blend of unrehearsed authenticity and a hunger for the truth.

Stewart shifts excitedly, like an only candidate for the top job. Griebenow thinks about addressing his client. but Stewart is way too eager to spill his narrative into the ears of the 'wedding guests'.

"I wanted to fuck my wife and she said no, and I found this whore and she wanted her money first, so I paid her and we fucked."

"Where was this?" Brian asks.

"At a school and she started to fucking hit me and I strangled her with her panties." Jordan checks her notes.

"Virginia Gysman." Dagbreek Primary. 3 October 1990."

"What?"

"Is her name Virginia Gysman?" Jordan clarifies

"Yes."

"Did you have normal sex with her?" Brian chirps in.

"No. I didn't know if she is a mother."

"So it was anal sex."

"After she was dead?"

Steward nods, "we went to the school place to fuck and she was angry and wanted to steal my money. The cunt hit me."

"Mercia Papenfus?" Jordan entices Stewart.

"She was a slut at the Red Lion. "She said her place to fuck is at the cricket park."

"Saint Georges? January 1991?"

"When I want to fuck she said I must pay before the fuck. We had a fight and I grabbed her neck and squeezed her and because I saw her eyes bulge. I couldn't stop. I fuck her again."

"Do you know a Georgina?" Jordan asks. "You were present at the crime scene when we found her?" Jordan shows a photo of Stewart amongst the spectators at the crime scene.

"Look at that! It's me. Can I keep it?"

Jordan takes a moment to calm down a bit before she proceeds.

"Did you kill her too?" Stewart nods. Jordan moves her finger to the dark figure in the photo. "Who is this man?"

"I can't say."

Stewart's response lands like a sucker punch, stealing the air from Jordan's lungs. She's left reeling, the shock of his words echoing in her ears.

I'm too gullible.

Frustration simmers beneath the surface, a slow burn that threatens to erupt. "Why not?"

"I just- cannot say!"

"Why the fuck not! Who is this man?"

Stewart looks at Brian and then at his lawyer.

"My client doesn't want to respond." Griebenow interjects.

"It's not that," Stewart responds.

Anger tightens its grip, Jordan's voice cuts through the tension. "Then what is it? Who is this man? Is he your watcher?" Her words are sharp, a demand for truth. Once the actor in control of the narrative, she finds herself on a stage where the script has unraveled into a web of deception and intrigue.

"I don't know him. That's why I can't say!" Stewart snaps back.

The realization that it was lost in translation hits home, but it cuts as deep as truth's razor. Jordan collapses into her chair, relieved and elated. The room is silent, caught in the aftermath of her emotional outburst.

Then her laughter erupts. It's not the gentle trickle of amusement but a torrential downpour of hysteria. The sound reverberates, echoing through the space like a hailstorm clattering down on a tin roof. "Then why don't you say so? Are you sure?"

"Yes."

Her laughter is uncontrollable, a cascade of wild abandon that catches everyone off guard. Each peal of laughter is a raindrop in the storm, hitting the surface with an unpredictable rhythm. "So nobody's watching me?"

Brian watches her with a mix of surprise and curiosity. And then, unexpectedly, Stewart joins her in laughter. It starts with a hesitant chuckle, a small crack in his stoic demeanor. But soon, it transforms into a shared mirth forcing everyone to smile.

Eventually they pipe down, and Brian can continue. "Why did you remove the clothing from the scene?"

"Jesus, you cops are clever. I was watching the police at the first woman, and they looked for stuff on her dress."

As soon as Brian places the image of the victims mutilated corpses down on the table, the reality of this man's banality kicks in for Jordan.

"What happened to Georgina?"

Jordan tries to steady herself, but the room seems to tilt, a carnival ride spiraling out of control.

"She made me angry. Very angry. And I cut her stomach. And I did bite her. Her nipples- I swallowed it." Stewart rubs himself.

"You also cut her vagina. Why?" Brian asks.

"I wanted to know what a woman's frog tastes like."

The air turns stale. Jordan grips the edge of the chair, her knuckles turning white. Sweat beads on her forehead, and the taste of fear lingers on her tongue.

"Did you eat her flesh as well?"

"It tasted very different from other meat. I decided to cook it next time." The killer's eyes bore into hers, devoid of remorse, and a wicked smile plays on his lips. It's a macabre puppet show, and Jordan is the captive audience. She knows she can't stay here.

"And I stuck the knife in and out, in and out, and I put the knife in her cunt and cut her open."

Desperation claws at her, urging her to escape the nightmare that unfolds. The room spins faster, threatening to swallow her whole.

Jordan refuses to be a vessel for the darkness that lurks in the killer's words. With a swift, deliberate movement, she rises from her chair, the legs scraping against the floor like an eerie symphony.

Stewart grabs his groin and jumps up. "I need to piss." Something drops out of his pocket.

It's a piece of my hair extensions.

The officers start to remove Stewart. Jordan shuts her eyes tightly, as if blocking out the world might somehow erase the horror. Her hands instinctively rise to cradle her face. For a moment that stretches into eternity, she remains frozen, a statue carved from the purest essence of dread. The exit beckons like a distant beacon of escape, a portal to another reality. With a numb determination, she darts towards it, her body guided more by muscle memory than conscious thought.

-SEVENTY-

†

J ordan realizes that she has been driving on autopilot for a while. Highway hypnosis. She lifts her foot off the gas and rolls down the windows to let the air currents play harp with her hair.

SHE STOPS TO STROLL along the beach, where lovers walk hand in hand, happy boys are kicking a rugby ball, and little girls build sand castles and dreams.

Normal, healthy lives.

The air is infused with the scent of salt and seaweed, and the rhythmic lullaby of crashing waves creates a soothing backdrop to the vibrant scene. The sky erupts into a magnificent spectrum of vivid colors- a palette al la Sunset at San Giorgio Maggiore.

A mellow canvas blending raspberry blue into tangerine, fading to lemon, and dipping to a pomegranate horizon. Each hue seems to tell a story, a fleeting moment captured in the ethereal strokes of twilight. I should be writing this, not about the abyss.

She's torn between the serene beauty before her and the haunting thoughts that linger in the recesses of her mind. But for now, she lets herself be absorbed by the kaleidoscope above, the colors reflecting in her eyes, momentarily pushing away the shadows.

She watches the sun immerse itself completely in the big bowl of black ink, a final burst of fiery brilliance before surrendering to the night. As she turns to leave, the sand beneath her feet whispers a soft farewell.

She drives back, the cool breeze tousling her hair, and she cranks up the radio to full volume when Steven Tyler starts belting out a hit song. The music becomes the soundtrack to her journey, the lyrics weaving through the wind, merging with the rhythmic hum of tires on pavement.

I could stay awake, just to hear you breathing.
Watch you smile, while you are sleeping.
While you're far away and dreaming

When she gets to her hotel, she'll change the airline tickets again. It's time to leave this Godforsaken place. It's time to go home.

Nobody to save but myself.

-SEVENTY-ONE-

†

With trembling fingers, David removes an envelope from his jacket's breast pocket. He counts out another grand and places the money close to him on the Blackjack table. The faint purple die stains on the edges of some of the notes are barely visible.

He wipes his sweaty palms on his trousers. The dealer slides a card across the table, and David's heart pounds in his chest. A ten. He exhales, relieved. The blackjack gods seem to be on his side, at least for this round.

With a deep breath, he signals for another card. An eight. The tension rises. He does the math in his head, calculating the risk.

Hit or stand?

His mind races as he battles the uncertainty that hangs over the table like a thick fog. In the end, he chooses to hit. A queen. Bust.

David clenches his jaw, frustration bubbling within him. He knows that it's time to cash out, but whether it's the adrenaline or his debt holding him at the table, is unsure.

Just one big win, then he'll call it a day.

"Place your bets."

The dealer deals. Ten of hearts. The dealer stands on eighteen. David raises a finger, he needs another hit.

The dealer supplies.

The junky has the jitters

He plays the card that has been dealt.

He flat lines. It's the Jack of Spades.

The floor gives way and vertigo overpowers David.

Fuck-it!

He steadies himself against the table. He can't leave.

I need to win some of my money back.

But as he reaches for more hard currency, the manager, flanked by security detail, discreetly taps him on the shoulder and requests that David step away from the table. He fists a wad of cash.

"Mr. Worth, I am Jack Bloom, the manager. Please come up to my office." It's a command, not a request.

David tries to compose himself. One of the burly men in black, steadies David as he follows Jack.

-SEVENTY-TWO-

†

B rian meets Jordan as soon as she parks her car.

"I am sorry." She says, getting out of the vehicle.

"I am glad you are okay. I was worried. Let's go in."

"I was freaking out. The fact that he gets turned on by his evil, revolting deeds. He is so fucking sick!"

They reach the kitchen. Brian points to the coffee maker and Jordan to the wine. He pours. She takes a seat.

"He looks me in the eyes and I can see his perverse mind reliving every stab and cut. I just can't do this. I can't write this story. Who wants to read this? It's fucking insanity!"

Brian joins her with two glasses. "Good. That is what we decided in the beginning."

"Baby, you should have warned me. David and you. You went on about the abyss and it sounded intriguing, even adventurous."

"I-."

"You should have spelled it out. But this is fucking hell."

"I tried to- because of your history. But you ignored me, you and David."

"My history? What does my past have to do with this sick fuck?"

"The consequence of trauma is learning to suppress emotional impulses."

"Meaning?"

"Why do you box, Jordan?"

"I told you already!"

"Boxing is a sport where you get hit in the face and where you defend yourself against an onslaught. It holds very little appeal to most women."

Jordan gets up. "What are you saying, Brian?"

"Your father was aggressive. I remember the bruises on David. I have seen the guys you chose. You have perfected the way to cover bruises with foundation and a smile."

"Never again."

"Still, that stained your soul. So you resist me."

Jordan paces around. "I have always tried to heal *that* dysfunctional stray. I am petrified of repeating my past. Trauma is the force that keeps me pushing for a better life. And if that is messed up-? I'll never belong to any man again."

"And together with your phobias it-"

"You arsehole! You fooled me into getting information from this sick fuck. You knew he would open up and confess to me. You study them and you studied me."

Brian scoffs as he stands up and that seems to add fuel to Jordan's inferno.

"I realized today that your job is a slow poison- That is what is killing all of you. Not David's divorce nor your girlfriend's death."

That hit where she intended to.

Brian turns his back on her.

"You are surrounded by all these, this macabre, theater of fucking death!" She continues. "You never get away from it. You stay in this place- with all these murders because you find some sort of perverted catharsis-"

"Jordan, stop it."

"Then why don't you immigrate? Why do you stay?"

"Because this is my home, if we all leave what then?"

"Do you think you can save them all? You can't save all the Harrys! We can't find this girl! Cheryl is right. Not even God can save her.

Nothing and nobody can! Except for the crazy fucker and he is getting off on it. You have this intellectual addiction to listen to every mental Mariner, just to feel like you stared down the monsters of the abyss. But in the end, the deck remains littered with the dead."

Jordan storms out, Brian follows her to the car.

"Well, for your information detective, I have no regrets only gratitude, because every fucking arsehole who ever scared me, has only made me the hard-punching bitch I am today!"

Jordan slams the door and speeds off, leaving Brian standing with his hands in his pockets.

-SEVENTY-THREE-

†

Jordan is not even upset that another piece of hair extension has fallen out. Tonight is not the night for petty concerns; it's a night for losing oneself in the hedonistic embrace of the moment.

Men in dark suits move through the crowd like predators in search of elusive prey. Jordan, however, remains untouched by their silent advances. Their whispered conversations and furtive glances slide off her like rain on a well-waxed coat. Not even the figure comfortably nestled in the shadows manages to stir a flicker of interest. He leans against the wall, a silhouette of mystery, a face hidden beneath the brim of a hat, a Heineken bottle cradled in his hand.

She lifts a shot glass to her lips; the burn down her throat is a reminder that, for tonight at least, she's the master of her own unraveling destiny. And then, like a serendipitous twist in a story, Cheryl appears at her side. A splash of vibrant red against the muted hues of the bar, she embodies the vivacity that Jordan's night was missing. Cheryl orders another round without a word, and the tequilas materialize like magic potions.

"This shit will get to you."

"You don't have a dick that you need to fuck someone over with, do you?"

"I get that sister." Cheryl laughs. She orders a whiskey.

Jordan turns around and points to the dark man.

"The guy in the photograph," Jordan scoffs. Cheryl turns to check the guy out.

"No, that's not him," Cheryl insists. The man clearly feels intimidated. He finishes his beer, pays, and leaves. Jordan couldn't be bothered. She bums a cigarette from Cheryl, lights up, and sucks the tar into her bronchi.

Fuck, that's good.

"So, what happened to you?" Cheryl prods.

"Today? I lost it."

"I mean, why?"

"We were at the bowling club for a braai."

Cheryl is confused. "What do you mean?"

"The motivation behind me leaving. Isn't that what you asked?"

"Continue."

Jordan's mood turns somber. "I was about sixteen. Our adoptive sister was eight months pregnant. We were celebrating at the bowling club when four armed thugs stormed into the clubhouse to rob the place," she says, her voice carrying the weight of the memories.

"But that wasn't enough for them. They struck my mum with the rifle-, struck her teeth out, and broke her jaw. You could see the unfettered hatred in their eyes." A stray light reflects off the bar mirror, casting eerie shadows across Jordan's face, accentuating the gravity of her words. She steels herself to continue.

"Then they forced my sister to the floor," Jordan says, her eyes distant as she relives the scene. "I'll never forget the fear in her eyes, the desperate plea for mercy. But mercy was a foreign concept to those men. They were ruthless, driven by something darker than mere greed. They wanted us all to witness this brutal rape and then rape of every woman in that room." Jordan's eyes well up.

"Don't worry, the one man laughed, you'll all get a chance to get some cock!"

"God!"

"I can't describe the absolute terror that we experienced."

Jordan gulps before she continues. "Out of nowhere, an armed security guard intervened. They exchanged gunfire before the men fled. The brave guard died, as well as the soon-to-be mother and her baby. His name is Michael and my sister's name is Mary."

Cheryl resists the need to grab and hold Jordan. It's as if the room itself absorbs her sorrow.

"They didn't just rob us of money and possessions that night," Jordan whispers, her voice cracking with emotion, "they robbed us of our sense of security, our trust in humanity. Every creak of a door or distant sound became a reminder of that horrifying night. It changed me, scarred me in ways that can't be seen but are deeply felt."

Jordan reaches for a handkerchief. "To this day Mum has never spoken about it."

"Neither has David. Jesus."

"Well, fuck that. I am out of this place by tomorrow night!"

"I am sorry to see you go."

"You said that God doesn't care about the world? Maybe even less when you are African. You should move to Australia or the USA. Save yourself for a change."

Cheryl snubs her fag. "I am too Western for Africa and not poor enough to be seen as a refugee by Europe. I can't afford American citizenship or Australia. We are fucked by history."

"I never thought of it that way!"

"I am African, despite my skin color and these are my people, despite their shade. If I ever leave, it will be for a good reason, but simply walking away without trying to make a positive impact- That's not me."

"People need people?"

Cheryl sings a line. "*We are the scatterlings of Africa*. We belong to the land, the land does not belong to us. I must change someone else's life so that mine can have value."

"Fuck that is beautiful. Can I use it someday?"

"It's yours." Their laughter dissipates into the bar's smog and order more shots.

"I'm gonna share a little something with you," Cheryl says without looking up from her glass. The moment of silence which follows has Jordan turning on her chair.

"Yes?"

"I was still at school back in 1990. Cellié High. Thursday morning, 8 February, I'll never forget that day- I arrived at school very early.-"

"No!"

"Yip," Cheryl answers, "I saw the mangled body of little Monte Fiko- spread eagle. His contorted legs looked like they were broken in several places."

"How bizarre. I'm sorry.."

"Don't be. That was the day that I decided that I wanted to be a detective."

"And now you have the fucker locked up."

"Suspect. Officially. But his confession should change his status soon," Cheryl smiles.

"So, how did it go with you and that little wanker, after I left." Jordan taunts and they laugh again. Cheryl's infectious laughter draws the attention of every male in the place.

"He confessed to strangling that girl you discovered next to the wall, Katriena Claassen. Boasting in detail."

"Why did he stick the plastic in her mouth."

"To prevent her from screaming."

"And the graffiti on the wall?"

"Deliberate. Because he believes women steal when they sell pussy for money."

"That what I told Brian." Suddenly, the sound of his name feels foreign to Jordan.

"He doesn't want to continue until you are present."

"Fuck him. I am not his biographer."

"I suspect that he is keeping Wuané somewhere."

"Cheryl, if I do this, I will never return from the abyss. I am sorry for Wuané, but I am not as strong as you. I am sure she is safe somewhere. He won't hurt her."

Jordan pays for the drinks. "I need a lift." Cheryl grabs her keys and finishes what's left in her glass. Jordan takes her by the arm. "I'll call the boys from the airport. Please don't say anything."

"Brian?"

"I don't want to think about that tonight."

-SEVENTY-FOUR-

†

B rian steps into Colonel Claassen's office to find the colonel sitting on the edge of his desk and David relegated to a chair in the corner, looking somber.

"Brian, thank you for coming in," Colonel Claassen begins, gesturing towards an empty chair. Brian dismisses the offer with a wave of his hand.

"No problem Colonel, how can I assist?"

The colonel takes a deep breath, his gaze unwavering. "There is no other way, but to give it to you straight. David has confessed to taking money from the police evidence store. He was apprehended with the money in the casino tonight, and he will plead 'no contest.'" Brian's eyes narrow in disbelief. "What money are we talking about?"

"That is the money that David recovered from the armored car heist."

"Are you guys shitting me?" Brian says, bemused. Claassen remains stoic. "Charges will be brought. That is a given, but because David has made some serious breakthroughs this week with the Wilken murders, it could jeopardize these cases. So, we will wait until the Wilken investigation has been concluded, before we proceed with prosecution. The casino agreed."

"Thank you, sir," David says.

Brian runs a hand through his hair, a sense of disbelief lingering. "So, what's the next move?"

"We need you to clean up the mess and salvage what's left of our reputation. The press is going to have a field day with this, and we can't afford any more damage."

"I'll do whatever it takes, Colonel."

"You boys better find Benjamin Mathews and Wuané Wilken and fast before any harm comes to them," Claassen says as he leaves.

Brian pulls David up by the hand. "Let's go."

As they make their way through the CID offices, David sells his version of events.

"When the judge threw the case out, I was pissed. Then Iggi came and stuck his ugly fucking face in mine and told me how fucking stupid I was for not taking his bribe. They offered me a million to make the docket disappear. I realized that money could solve all my problems. It was the reason I lost my wife and daughter."

They reach Brian's vehicle. "I took a little of the cash from the evidence room to gamble with, hoping that I would hit the mother load. I always planned on putting the money back, and no one would be the wiser."

Brian starts the car. "How much did you take?"

"I started with ten grand and then another ten, then it just escalated as I tried to win it all back."

"Is your car still at the casino?" Brian checks with David. David nods. "All in all, I took about a hundred and sixty grand. I didn't blow it all. I'll give the rest back tomorrow."

"That will help your case and the fact that you owned up to your mistakes."

"I came close at times to winning big, but fuck it, lady luck evaded me every time."

There is a moment of silence before David speaks again. "You know, I had this belief that only criminals break the law. Fuck, it is easy to step over the line. Especially as a cop."

"You can't take back a bullet once it's fired, brother," Brian assures him. "Okay, but let's focus on tomorrow."

THE DIM GLOW OF FLICKERING streetlights casts long shadows across the casino's deserted parking lot. Brian's car purrs to a stop next to David's vehicle.

David checks his pockets for his keys before getting out and moving around to Brian's window. "We recovered DNA from Henry. The team is working twenty-four-seven on all the case files to which he confessed," Brian says.

"That's fantastic. Let's stay focused."

"I need to talk to Jordan. Stewart won't give up the girl to us."

"Give her space- she'll come around."

"Let's stay focused," Brian says and drives off.

The chill of the night air settles around David as he walks to his parked car. The rhythmical echo of his footsteps is the only sound accompanying him to this part of the desolate parking bay.

Just as he reaches for his car door, a voice pierces the stillness behind him. "Hallo Lanie David."

David snaps around, his hand instinctively going for the firearm at his side. The beam of a distant florescent tube spills just enough light to reveal two figures emerging from obscurity. To his astonishment, the silhouettes resolve into the unmistakable forms of teenagers.

In the shadows, a girl stands with an air of mischief- it's Nimo. Beside her is a boy, none other than Benjamin Mathews.

-SEVENTY-FIVE-

†

The door shuts with a muted thud as Jordan sinks into the plush leather seat of the hotel's town car. The chauffeur nods respectfully before circling the vehicle to take his place behind the wheel.

Through the tinted windows, she steals a final glance at Shark Rock Pier. Its silhouette is etched against the horizon, a tranquil seascape painted in hues of teal and azure. Leaning back, Jordan releases a wistful sigh, her gaze fixed on the disappearing vista.

The town car glides away, the driver weaving through coastal roads at Jordan's behest. Jordan's fingers tap nervously on her phone. The familiar weight of the device is both a lifeline and a harbinger of difficult conversations.

She unlocks the phone, navigates to Brian's contact, and hesitates. Her voice is steady, yet tinged with a vulnerability she can't conceal.

"Brian," she begins, the resonance of his name catching in her throat. "I'm sorry, but I can't do this in person." The confession lingers in the air, heavy with the weight of unspoken truths. "I'm on my way to the airport," she continues, the road slipping away beneath the car's tires.

"I'll call you once I'm back in the States. Please don't be mad." Jordan takes a deep breath before uttering words she never thought she'd say: "I've never been a quitter, but this- This is a dragon I can't slay like you."

The admission hangs in the air, a confession of vulnerability and the acknowledgment of her own limitations.

"I'm sorry, Brian," she concludes, her sincerity echoing through the airwaves. "I never meant to hurt you." With those words, she ends the message, the silence that follows amplifying the gravity of her decision.

The vehicle jerks to a halt, the sudden stop jolting Jordan from her idle contemplation.

Her eyes shift to the unfolding drama outside the car window. A man, donned in a stylish cream suit, strolls across the road, engrossed in a conversation on his phone. His self-absorbed stride disrupts the traffic flow, drawing a grumble from the chauffeur. The man brings the intersection to a complete standstill.

But Jordan's compassion lies with the hapless boy being dragged along by his father. In the commotion, the boy dropped his toy truck and a bag of jelly beans. The ignorant man is oblivious to this. His son tries to garner his attention, but he just jerks the lagging boy's arm again.

Then a street child, keenly observant, rushes forward. With a kind heart, he retrieves the toy truck and runs to return it to the crying boy.

However, the man is far from grateful. Disgust clouds his face at the street child's lewd appearance. He grabs the truck, shuns the child, throws the toy on the sidewalk, and shatters it. Then he raises his son by the arm and spanks him for crying.

Meanwhile, the street child scurried back to where the spilled jelly beans lie scattered. He squats down and, like a rooster, he pecks up the beans that escaped the wrath of passing tires.

The chauffeur, attuned to Jordan emotional response, breaks the silence. His voice addresses her reflection in the rear-view mirror.

"I am a grandfather myself."

"I don't have children."

"Yet your maternal instinct is strong," he smiles, "Madam, do you know about the Benjamin Mathews boy that disappeared?"

"Yes, I do."

"Then I may have fantastic news for you," the smiling

man announces, his words hanging in the air. "He has been found, unharmed."

-SEVENTY-SIX-

†

The door swings open, and Brian storms in, a dark cloud of frustration trailing behind him like a storm. His brow is furrowed, and his is jaw clenched as he zeroes in on David. Without a word, he seizes David's arm and pulls him away from Cheryl.

"I just got a message on my machine from Jordan. She's on her way back home," Brian spits out, his voice a mix of disbelief and anger.

David's eyes widen, a surge of panic coursing through him. "What? Why?"

Brian's frustration boils over. "Well, maybe it's because her arse-of-a-brother coaxed her into believing that she is mentally indestructible and strong enough to interview a psychopath!"

David shakes his head in disbelief, his mind racing to comprehend the sudden turn of events. "I'm sorry, but you know as well as I do that she was the only person who could unlock this guy's mouth. The only solid DNA we have was taken off Henry. We owe it all to Jordan."

Brian knows the truth when he hears it. "Fuck."

"Without his testimony, all three of us would've been left counting bodies."

"You're right. I know."

"I'll phone my sister to check if she's okay." David is about to leave when Brian asks, "What is the latest on Iggi?"

"What do you mean?"

"He was killed a couple of days ago."

"What? How?"

"Gunned down in his driveway," Brian answers, demanding an honest response. "Do you know anything about this?"

"Hey, fuck you, Brian. I made one mistake, but I don't kill people."

Brian relents. "Okay. I needed to check."

Two officers escort a moody Stewart in and cuff him to the chair. He watches Cheryl make final adjustments to her audio equipment and snorts in derision when she says, "We are ready everyone!"

"Where is Jordan?" Stewart asks.

"She is not available today. She is not feeling well. She'll watch the tape tonight," Cheryl bluffs.

Stewart struggles up. "Take me back," he instructs his lawyer. Brian tries to salvage the sinking vessel. "We found Benjamin Mathews. He's unscathed."

"And so you thought I lied? Take me back." Stewart is adamant, and his legal council complies. A uniformed officer moves in and Stewart starts shuffling towards the door. Jordan, disheveled but determined, comes storming through the door and past a stunned Stewart, her eyes ablaze with a sense of urgency.

Without a moment's hesitation, she seizes Brian's hand and yanks him towards the hallway in a whirlwind of motion. The door creaks closed behind them, leaving the room in a stunned silence. In the hallway, the ambient sounds of the bustling station surround Jordan and Brian. "Where did you find Benjamin?"

"The girl- Nimo brought him to David. He was hungry and missed his mother."

"Exactly. A child needs a parent, and if Wuané is not with her mother, she is with him. And if he's locked up?"

"Then she's left to her own devices!"

"As God is my witness, I'll beat it out of him," she says. Brian is both amused and overjoyed to see her. "You're brave, Jade." She manages a smile. "I am fucking petrified. Every time I am in this man's presence- I lie, in the hope of keeping that girl alive." Her eyes become moist.

"I believe in you, Jade."

As they reenter the room, all eyes gravitate toward Jordan. Without acknowledging their speculative gazes, she strides purposefully back to her usual seat, a veneer of calm concealing the turmoil within.

Stewart, reclines in his chair, a sardonic smile playing on his lips. "I thought that you forgot about me," he chuckles, his voice laced with a disturbing mix of confidence and mockery. Jordan is not in the mood to roll snot snakes with this guy.

"When were you in our house?"

"I was never in your house." Stewart leaps back on defense. Jordan holds up a hair extension. Stewart is caught completely off guard. "Then where the fuck did you get this?"

"It fell out of your hair."

"Where?"

"The one time I saw you here and it was in the sand too, after you left."

Jordan is mortified.

He is fucking obsessed!

Jordan's gaze meets Stewart's, her expression unreadable. She lowers her voice to make maximum impact.

"Wuané must be very lonely when her daddy is not there at night. She must be cold and hungry by now." Stewart's legs start to gyrate.

"You will not be going back to Wuané for a while. Depending on what the judge says. Do you understand?"

It takes a moment for Stewart to grasp the gravity of Jordan's words. The reality of the situation settles in, and he nods in agreement, a sense of unease creeping into his eyes.

"Please take me to Wuané before someone else finds her," Jordan urges, her plea filled with desperation. "Don't you miss her?"

Stewart's mood swings from resignation to sudden enthusiasm. "Get us a couple of cokes. Who has the nicest car?"

Brian, sensing the shift in the atmosphere, steps out and calls a constable over and hands him cash to buy sodas. The young man nods and heads out to fulfill the request. Then Brian pulls Jordan into the hallway, his expression serious.

"Talk to me," he says, his concern evident. Jordan leans in and kisses his cheek, a bittersweet gesture of gratitude.

"All I seem to do these days is apologize to you. Only now have I come to understand the depth of this man's depravity."

"You need to give me more than an apology. I need an explanation, and I need to know where I fit in."

Jordan places a finger on his lips. "Apologizing doesn't come easy, so let me. I thought that by beating poverty, the mother of all diseases, it would heal me. Money only makes us arrogant. Especially me. I don't need medicine. I need purpose."

"You were not all wrong, Jade. I can't save anyone."

"Baby, you saved me."

"That's not what I expected to hear. But I love it."

"Do you believe that we can save at least one child? I do."

"Without you, we wouldn't have the chance to."

Jordan smiles. "Don't gloat it's not becoming," Brian jokes, "and you did it without spending cash."

"Let's get Wuané back to her mother. I'll go with Cheryl."

"Promise me you won't put yourself in harm's way again."

"Let's just see what this day brings." She gives him an assuring look.

The metallic click of handcuffs echos through the sterile hallway as two police officers secure Stewart's wrists behind his back. Final equipment checks create a brief pause in the action, an interlude of anticipation. Jordan snatches her leather notebook and pencils, ready to document the unfolding drama. Cheryl stuff camera tapes and batteries into a bag and slings the Betamax over her shoulder.

Meanwhile, David, the conductor of this decisive performance, swiftly coordinates with a police photographer to be on standby.

The quartet, armed with their tools of observation, joins Stewart's entourage congregating in the hallway. As they exit the building, the atmosphere thickens with tension and a sense of impending revelation. Yet, inside David's office, perched on Stewart's vacated chair, is a plastic doll meant for a little girl.

-SEVENTY-SEVEN-

†

Cheryl fumbles for her keys as Stewart is placed in the back of David's car. Brian rides shotgun.

Stewart's voice slices through the quiet, derailing Jordan's train of thought. It's not the voice of a cold blooded strangler, but rather that of an excited child on the cusp of a long-awaited adventure.

"Come ride with us," he calls out, gesturing towards the empty seat beside him, his usual stoic demeanor replaced by something unsettling.

Her hand hovers over the door handle. Should she heed the warning bells clamoring for caution, or accept Stewart's offer in order to gain crucial intel and trust?

Stewart calls out repeatedly,"Jordan! Come ride with us!" She turns to Cheryl. "What do you think?"

"I think you should be honest with yourself?"

"What? I am talking about riding in a car with him."

"And I am talking about deciding between what you want and what you believe you can handle."

"Meaning?"

"Every time that you think that you are losing something, it manifests itself through confusion, anger or denial. Nobody is taking anything from you, especially not Brian."

"I know."

"It's unhealthy to disengage. It's torture to isolate someone."

"I won't forgive myself if I don't try to find that little girl."

"You know he'll support you, but you need to deal with the consequences. Can you?"

Jordan ponders the conversation. "I've been to the abyss, seen the dead, worn the albatross- All that's left is to reach the harbor. Can you understand that?"

Cheryl lights a cigarette. "And so she came to understand the rime..."

"I won't run again."

"No matter what the mariner has to show or tell?"

With a steely resolve, Jordan makes her choice. Whether it leads to salvation or damnation remains to be seen. And as she steps closer to the idling vehicle, she braces herself for the inevitable descent into the depths of uncertainty. There is a concerned expression on Brian's face, as he starts to vacate the front seat, but she holds the door. "I'll sit in the back- I need you to trust me."

Jordan holds the ace and she knows it. With both arms, Jordan leans against the roof of the car, looks the killer square in the eyes and says, "Before I get into this car I want to know, where do we get Wuané?"

The answer is short, simple and clear. Yet, it's not what anyone expects.

"Take me to the Hotel."

Stewart is all smiles, when the convoy starts moving. "Coke in a car trip. That must be what a real date feels like!"

-SEVENTY-EIGHT-

†

After a drive where nobody spoke, except Stewart, the police convoy arrive at Jordan's Hotel, He felt compelled to share the intimate details of his murderous exploits again. Jordan can't wait to break away from the squawking albatross.

I wanted him to talk, now I want him to shut the fuck up!

Stewart directs them towards the parking area behind the hotel, where the various teams then park, and regroup for a strategy session, before Stewart is brought to them.

As a green Mazda 323 approaches the team, they can't help but notice its battered-down appearance. The paint has lost its luster, scratches and dents cover the exterior and the cloud it emits is a clear indication that the engine is on its last legs.

A woman in her seventies gets out, coughs up a pound of phlegm and lights a cigarette. Brian excuses himself. "Guys, just give me a minute." He walks over to the car, speaks to the woman and then escorts her to where Stewart is waiting.

"Stewart, I want you to meet someone." The woman looks at Stewart's confused expression for a while before she places her hands on the sides of his face.

"Hello, Stewart." She gives him an uncomfortable hug. "I am Alice, I'm your mother."

Stewart watches the old woman in disbelief.

"I saw you on TV, maybe you are famous now."

"Are you my mother? My mommy?"

"Look, I want to tell you, I have never abandoned you." She ashes her cigarette. "One day your father just came and took you away."

"Mommy!"

"And when I found you, I was so happy. I brought you sweeties, but you wanted to stay with Doep. You didn't want to come out from under the table. I didn't know what to do. It seemed like he liked you."

"Mommy, Mommy!" Stewart sobs like a child.

"But I have never stopped thinking about you. You are still my boy. Okay?"

"Yes, Mommy!"

"The detective told me that you have Wuané. You must bring her to meet her granny."

Stewart nods and wipes the mucus from his nose. "Yes Granny," he jokes.

"I will come to the court every day. Okay? You are always my boy no matter what. You can phone me any time. They have my number. Okay?"

"Yes, Mommy!"

"But I want to see my granddaughter. Okay?"

"Okay."

"I will speak to you later."

As the woman leaves, Stewart dries his eyes with his sweater. He is suddenly in high spirits. Jordan feels perforated by the emotional shards of the inconvenient encounter and is uncertain of how to proceed.

"I have never called anyone Mommy before!" He waves as Alice's car departs. Then he turns to Jordan. "Come."

Stewart walks towards the fence of the parking area where the veld starts. "Jordan only."

Brian responds. "Hell no."

Jordan looks at Brian and David for guidance. Brian walks up to Jordan, he places his hands on her shoulders. David and Cheryl encircle her. "Jordan, this is crossing the line!" Cheryl tells her.

"If we can't rescue anyone, then we have wasted it all. Let me bring her home." Stewart climbs through a hole in the fence and waits for Jordan to follow. "Let's go. Jordan"

"Hug your brother," Brian instructs Jordan.

"Why?"

Brian turns Jordan to face David. As she puts her arms around David's neck, she understands Brian's intention. He presses up against her back and shoves a cold, hard item into the back of her waistband. She realizes that he has armed her with his .38 Special. He straightens her jacket to conceal the revolver.

"Don't hesitate to shoot. We'll be right behind you."

Jordan climbs through the hole in the fence. She joins Stewart and they disappear into the dense brush, at the same time that the sun starts it's decent over the horizon.

Soon it will be pitch black.

-SEVENTY-NINE-

†

"**A**lmost two minutes," Brian says, sliding a live round into the chamber of his Beretta. He is fully aware of the brevity of the risk he is taking. Should Jordan get injured or worse-

He adjusts his earpiece, checks the radio signal and briefs the uniformed officers again. "Two minutes before you start following and keep a comfortable distance."

Cheryl and David are locked and loaded. Brian takes the lead as they pour through the fence.

He spent hours in the bush with his father and today he'll employ all the hunting, stalking and tracking skills he picked up on the hunt. Taking to heart his dad's words, *"Any skill you gain today will be spent tomorrow,"* he sets off to protect Jade.

JORDAN'S SENSES ARE heightened for any signs of danger, to the degree of an animal navigating the Serengeti. She is attuned to every movement that Stewart makes. Judging by the speed at which Stewart navigates the path, while his hands are cuffed, it's evident that he knows this route very well. He stops suddenly.

Jordan keeps her distance. He listens attentively to hear if they are being followed. Her heart is racing. The sweat pearls on her brow.

Nothing.

Satisfied, Stewart starts walking again.

The abrasive brush tears at Jordan's jacket and the path is rocky.

I should have changed shoes.

THE TRIO MOVES CAUTIOUSLY, yet rapidly along the pathway, slightly hunched over, guns holstered, when Brian holds up a fist and they halt. They can pick up the faint sounds of twigs snapping ahead. It means that they are gaining on Jordan's position.

The tension is palpable. Brian lowers his hand and they are on the move again, steering through the underbrush, every step taken with care.

AS JORDAN STEPS INTO a small clearing in the veld, her eyes fall upon the makeshift shelter constructed beneath and tied to the thin tree. It can provide little shade, of that she's sure.

The corrugated sheeting, fragmented road signs, and black plastic lining forms a patchwork structure held together by rusted wire and frayed rope. The scene was one of improvised survival, a stark contrast to the natural beauty of the surrounding landscape.

As she walks among the debris, her gaze shifts from the discarded polystyrene food containers to the squashed beer cans.

Jordan can't help but feel a pang of empathy. Turning to Stewart, she voiced her question, her tone a mix of curiosity and concern. "Is this where you live now?"

Stewart picks up a piece of nylon rope and plays with it.

"Do you like it?"

"For how long?"

He chooses a rock as a chair and sits down to watch the sunset. "A lot of years. I like to look down at Happy Valley." He points to the recreational park below their vantage point. "Daddy used to take me and we were always happy there."

Jordan detects a slight smell of feces lingering but can't see anything resembling a toilet. Inside the shelter, she observes a weathered, dark green tarpaulin. It's covered in red, yellow and blue paint stains.

"Come sit here. And we'll watch the sun drop into the sea." He invites her closer.

"I'll stand, then I can see it better."

"Every evening we sit here and we talk about- And I never had a daddy or a mummy- Until now!" He burst out laughing.

A startled Jordan almost reaches for the gun.

"I want to be a good dad, but I am fucked up and I do fucked-up things. Maybe if Mommy was rich like you, she would not have left and I would not be so fucked. Hey?"

Even though more than half of the sun has sunk below the horizon, it still sets the cloudscape ablaze, with the fiery colors of an apocalypse.

"If I tell the truth I won't go to jail for long hey? And in the jail, there will be doctors to make me better and I can live with mommy and bring my kids there and I won't want to hurt people."

Jordan is stunned. "Do you have more children?"

Stewart nods. "I won't smoke Mandrax anymore."

"That sounds good. Is Wuané in the hotel?"

He ignores her petition. "You are so lucky to be rich and famous."

Jordan starts to tremble. "You have more than me. You have children who loves you more than anything."

Stewart breaks down and sobs. "I can't give them food or toys or anything."

Jordan zips up her jacket. "What do you think Wuané needs? She needs her mother, feeling safe and loved, more than money?"

Stewart starts stacking up wood for a fire. "And everybody loves you. And it's better to have food." He strikes a match and lights the wood. Then he blows until there are ample flames. The sun finally drags the sky's orange fabric with it into the depths of the ocean. Stewart's fire is now the only source of light.

"Where is your child?"

"She's here. We have both been on TV now, me and you."

"Do you think Wuané wants you to be famous?"

"Maybe."

"Do you think that the people who read my books love me? They love the facade. And many people hate me because of my success." Jordan realizes that she is talking just to calm her nerves.

This was an idiotic idea!

Stewart jumps up. "And Lynn calls the police when I talk to Wuané and she fucking hates me and so we come here to talk and she is always hungry because they don't feed her!" As he moves towards Jordan, she backs away.

"Listen to me. All that matters, is Wuané."

Stewart picks up a tin canister. From it, he takes out his Okapi knife. "And when I go to jail, I want you to have my knife."

"You have a knife?" Jordan says out loud hoping that her rescue party receives the info.

"My dad gave it to me. It's all I have- That I can give you."

"Is Wuané with people in the hotel?"

"I beg food from them and we come to look at the sunset, then she sleeps and I hold her."

"Where is she now?"

"She came to me and she said to me that her step-dad was beating them and I think Michael was molesting her." Stewart opens the knife's blade. Jordan's hand moves towards her back, feeling for the handle of the revolver.

"Stewart, where is Wuané?"

"I looked to see if she was still a virgin," he seethes.

Jordan shouts. "Where are you hiding Wuané?"

Stewart looks down at the green tarpaulin in the shelter. Jordan follows his gaze.

Did he build a bunker?

She slowly lifts the corner of the tarp. Stewart starts fidgeting with the knife as he slowly moves closer to her. In the dim light, he can make out a bulge at the back of her jacket. His shadow falls over Jordan. She drops the canvas and backs away. Stewart holds the knife out for Jordan to take. Jordan so desperately wants to reach for the comfort of her gun, but perishes the idea. "Is Wuané under the tarp?"

Stewart nods.

"Did you dig a bunker?"

Stewart shakes his head and moves towards Jordan. Brian has had enough. The trio step into the clearing and move purposely toward Stewart. Guns drawn.

"Drop your knife, Stewart."

"It's not my knife, it's Jordan's." He still holds out the knife for Jordan to take. Remembering the tense harbor stand-off, Jordan takes a step closer, grabs the Okapi and steps out of striking distance again. There is a moment of inactivity, then David orders Stewart to sit down. He obeys. Jordan moves back towards the shelter.

She lifts the tarp and instantly her eyes well up. She sinks to her knees.

"Wuané!" She drops the tarp.

Brian and Cheryl rush closer. David covers Stewart. Brian peels back the tarp to reveal the badly decomposed body of Wuané. There is a dark patch of hair on a skinless skull and a silk stocking is still tied around the neck of the skeleton.

Her clothes are folded beside her and a collection of discarded animal bones lies scattered around her body.

"Don't cry Jordan," Stewart tries to pacify her, "she is happy with Jesus now."

Jordan reaches for the revolver. She draws it from her belt.

She lets it hang by her side.
She pulls the hammer back.
She lifts the weapon. She aims.
She so desperately wants to send Stewart to God-
But God doesn't want him.
Brian takes the revolver from Jordan's shaking hand.
Jade weeps.

-EIGHTY-

†

"Since then, at an uncertain hour,
That agony returns:
And till my ghastly tale is told,
This heart within me burns."
- Rime of the ancient mariner.

SANTA BARBARA. USA. 2003.

I should be outside not working.

But last week was the Old Spanish Days Festival, she had her break and now she needs to finish the final chapter of her novel.

I hate submission dates!

There is an 8mm film projector next to the computer, casting its frames against the wall where Jordan's book posters have been removed, temporarily. In the silent film, little boy Stewart frolics in the gardens of Happy Valley.

Jordan starts dictating into a microphone and as she speaks, her words are typed across the screen of her Mac.

"I guess that *if* we are all born equal, then it is all about *where* we are born equal."

Stewart is all smiles as Mister Wilken pushes him on the rides. "How does my place of birth, define the state of my soul, or my values in life? Are we then born either angels or fallen demons, according to the tectonic plate our feet hit first? The chronicles of Stewart, do not seem to find atonement in any Western heaven, nor in Eastern nirvana. It is the brutal stream of violent poverty, transferred from one generation to another, which perpetuates in an endless, relentless loop."

The film runs out. Jordan switches the projector off before she continues, "It seems that we have to swallow hell first, to get acquainted with heaven, that is, if we are allowed the opportunity to repent."

Brian enters with coffee, followed by the feisty two-year-old David. "Oh, mommy needs a hug." And she gets one.

"Come on, mommy needs to work. She can't play like we can." Brian teases. "Oh sod off," Jordan responds while stealing another kiss from her son. Brian grabs his boy, kisses his wife and the pair leave with a "Don't work too hard, Misses Harper."

Back to work.

"David repented his sin and received a sentence of ten months imprisonment in a single cell. He was, however, allowed to leave prison at times to conclude cases he'd been handling and in so doing, he sent other souls away to repent."

On the mantelpiece are several portraits of David and Cheryl on their respective wedding days. "David and Cheryl both got married, just not to each other. By then, they had established a food shelter for street kids. Nimo became a close friend and was rewarded with the responsibility of now managing the NPO venture while David works security detail in Africa."

Jordan stops to thread another spool of film through the projector. It's a film of Lynn and her baby girl playing in Petronella's rose garden.

Jordan dictates. "And so it would seem, that all those affected by this narrative, will only find catharsis by either retelling the tale or by listening, until The Ancient Mariner concludes his narration. Others may only find it in death."

Jordan reflects on her notes, she stirs the coffee before continuing. "In a strange twist, Lynn Havenga went strolling to the shops, when she was abducted and pulled into a vehicle by unknown assailants.

Her body was later discovered at the infamous Salt Pans. Her skull had been pulverized with a brick. The motive was never established. Maybe someone visited Stewart's sin on Wuané's mother? Must the sins of the fathers be the legacy of their children?"

Jordan hears her son's ecstatic laughter. She watches Brian and little David with envious eyes from the balcony. The little boy is all over his father.

"I shall forever marvel at my good fortune of discovering my purpose, my need above my want. I can only pledge to dispense love like October rain, upon my children, because I have seen the horror that abandonment produces and I desire to witness it no more."

Jordan turns to view the film of baby Wuané and Lynn.

"Like most nights, Stewart is crying in his prison cell. Tonight, he is again haunted by visitations of his victim's energy for they are his watchers. This I have come to know, from the letters I still receive regularly."

Stewart sits on the lawn, with Wuané climbing all over him, before the reel runs out. The recognizable sound of fluttering film and turning gears, signals the tedious task to change spools again, which Jordan does.

It takes patience and grit to be an author.

The last reel starts. On the screen, a young Stewart's family, is celebrating his birthday. His father hands him a gift. He tears it open. It's an Okapi knife.

"The law of the abyss is thus: When the aggressor is powerless to visit his aggression upon the vulnerable, he reverts back to being the victim. My incidental meeting with the Mariner has led me to inescapable truths: The first, is that crippling poverty remains the mother of all diseases and there is no saintly protection for the meek. The second may be harder to accept: We are all impacted by a stranger's child. Whether it's the boy like Stewart, or whether it's the man like Stewart."

"The Mariner, whose eye is bright,
Whose beard with age is hoar,
Is gone: and now the Wedding-Guest
Turned from the bridegroom's door.
He went like one that hath been stunned,
And is of sense forlorn:
A sadder and a wiser man,
He rose the morrow morn."

- The Rime of the Ancient Mariner

-EPILOGUE-

†

Stewart Wilken was charged with 10 counts of murder and 5 counts of sodomy. He was convicted of 7 counts of murder and 2 counts of sodomy.

Wilken received 7 life sentences.

He still writes letters from prison to his remaining children.

He applied for Parole in 2023 but was denied.

Don't miss out!

Visit the website below and you can sign up to receive emails whenever Johnny Taute publishes a new book. There's no charge and no obligation.

https://books2read.com/r/B-A-ULFEB-TZAYC

BOOKS 2 READ

Connecting independent readers to independent writers.

Also by Johnny Taute

Jelly Bean Effect

About the Author

Johnny Taute is a South African film producer, director, & screenplay writer. He started his career as a sergeant in the South African Police's Video Unit, filming violent crime scenes, riots, and human conflict videos.Johnny was instrumental in establishing a multi-media training unit at the Faculty of Health Sciences at the University of Pretoria to train graduate and post-graduate students. He is currently involved in feature films and documentary videos and has traveled the globe searching for human interest stories.

Milton Keynes UK
Ingram Content Group UK Ltd.
UKHW020646080324
439098UK00013B/398